"Are you lost?" Ben asked solemnly.

"Yes," Eden answered, a tremor in her voice.

"Me, too," he said.

He held out his hand, and she took it, letting him bring her inside. And when his arms went around her, she couldn't keep from making a small, needy sound.

Home, she thought, clinging to him hard.

"I don't know what's happening," she said. Her eyes searched his. "I don't—"

He stroked her cheek. "Maybe this—right now—is all there is for us," he said. "Maybe we can't have anything else."

About to cry, she pressed her face into his chest. "Then," she breathed, "we'll have to take what we can get...."

Dear Reader,

Happy New Year! We look forward to bringing you another year of captivating, deeply satisfying romances that will surely melt your heart!

January's THAT SPECIAL WOMAN! title revisits the Window Rock community for the next installment of Cheryl Reavis's FAMILY BLESSINGS miniseries. *Tenderly* is about a vulnerable young woman's quest to uncover her heritage—and the once-in-a-lifetime love she discovers with a brave Navajo police officer. Don't miss this warm, wonderful story!

It's a case of unrequited love—or is it?—in *The Nine-Month Marriage,* the first story in Christine Rimmer's delightful new series, CONVENIENTLY YOURS. This starry-eyed heroine can't believe her ears when the man she worships proposes a marriage—even if it's just for their baby's sake. And the red-hot passion continues when a life-threatening crisis brings a tempestuous couple together in *Little Boy Blue* by Suzannah Davis—book three in the SWITCHED AT BIRTH miniseries.

Also this month, fate reunites a family in *A Daddy for Devin* by Jennifer Mikels. And an unlikely duo find solace in each other's arms when they are snowbound together, but a secret threatens to drive them apart in *Her Child's Father* by Christine Flynn. We finish off the month with a poignant story about a heroine who falls in love with her ex-groom's brother, but her child's paternity could jeopardize their happiness in *Brother of the Groom* by Judith Yates.

I hope this New Year brings you much health and happiness! Enjoy this book and all our books to come!

Sincerely,

Tara Gavin
Senior Editor and Editorial Coordinator

Please address questions and book requests to:
Silhouette Reader Service
U.S.: 3010 Walden Ave., P.O. Box 1325, Buffalo, NY 14269
Canadian: P.O. Box 609, Fort Erie, Ont. L2A 5X3

CHERYL REAVIS

TENDERLY

Silhouette®

SPECIAL EDITION®

Published by Silhouette Books
America's Publisher of Contemporary Romance

To Tara Gavin:

Thank you for your always expert advice. Thank you for letting me whine when I need to. Most of all, thank you for letting me be me.

 SILHOUETTE BOOKS

ISBN 0-373-24147-X

TENDERLY

Copyright © 1998 by Cheryl Reavis

This edition published by arrangement with Harlequin Books S.A.

® and TM are trademarks of Harlequin Books S.A., used under license. Trademarks indicated with ® are registered in the United States Patent and Trademark Office, the Canadian Trade Marks Office and in other countries.

Printed in U.S.A.

CHERYL REAVIS,

award-winning short-story author and romance novelist who also writes under the name of Cinda Richards, describes herself as a "late bloomer" who played in her first piano recital at the tender age of thirty. "We had to line up by height—I was the third-smallest kid," she says. "After that, there was no stopping me. I immediately gave myself permission to attempt my *other* heart's desire—to write." Her Silhouette Special Edition novel *A Crime of the Heart* reached millions of readers in *Good Housekeeping* magazine. Both *A Crime of the Heart* and *Patrick Gallagher's Widow* won the Romance Writers of America's coveted RITA Award for Best Contemporary Series Romance the year they were published. *One of Our Own* received the Career Achievement Award for Best Innovative Series Romance from *Romantic Times* magazine. A former public health nurse, Cheryl makes her home in North Carolina with her husband.

Dear Reader,

My agent, Maureen Moran, and I have a running joke about The Padlocked Closet, a kind of mental vault wherein I keep my most persistent but bookless characters so they won't bother me until I can find them a plot to live in. Some of the historical ones, like Amanda Douglas and John Howe from *The Prisoner,* and Caroline Holt and Frederich Graeber from *The Bartered Bride,* stayed locked away for years. Others, like Eden Trevoy, barely saw the inside. From the moment she came to life in my imagination, I understood the task at hand. She had some very painful unfinished business to attend to, and I had to do a little matchmaking and finally bring home a lost child.

I could see right away that Eden was the kind of woman I most admire. Her strength had been born of necessity. As a little girl, she had suffered much because of the wrong turns and unhappy circumstances of the adults around her. But not only did she emerge with a Euripides brand of courage, the courage to "bear unflinchingly what heaven sends," she also had Thomas Carlyle's stout heart that is also warm and kind. A woman's heart, you see, is one that understands that life is what it is, and one can either stand and bemoan the most recent pitfall or one can try one's best to learn from it and move on. It's no wonder Ben Toomey fell in love with her, and I must tell you that he was *almost* as happy to have a book of his very own— with Eden—as I was to hear that she had been chosen to be this month's THAT SPECIAL WOMAN.

I sincerely hope you enjoy their story.

Cheryl Reavis

Chapter One

It took him the better part of a day to find the way into the arroyo. He had only been there once, when he was a boy, and while the terrain hadn't changed all that much, he had. All those years ago, he had navigated the narrow slit between the great rocks easily, but now he could barely fit himself into the small crevice that led to the place where he thought Edna Trevoy would be. He was reasonably certain that he had finally found the actual entrance, but the daylight was rapidly fading, and he decided that the path was too treacherous to attempt alone in the dark. He tried calling out to her, knowing that if she had indeed gone to the ledge and the wall where the spiral petroglyphs were, the sound of his voice would likely never penetrate the rocky overhang.

In spite of his sense of urgency, there was nothing to do but wait for somebody to catch up with him. As it was, he would have a lot of explaining to do. The entire time he'd been looking for this place, he had gone over and over in his mind how he would justify his being out here to the lieutenant. He had decided that he would say first that he'd gone on alone because he hadn't wanted to waste any more time. He would say that the whole situation was crazy, that he hadn't seen Professor Trevoy in years. He would say that there had to be some serious reason why she would tell people she was going to this almost inaccessible place in the big canyon and that the only other person who knew the way in was Navajo tribal police officer, Ben Toomey. She'd apparently been very specific about that part, leaving her colleagues to think that he had gone with her.

They'd been so certain that, when she didn't return after two days, they'd called the tribal police to find out if said officer had given anyone a specific itinerary.

He had been happily minding his own business when the call came in—no, actually, he'd been minding the business of a very busty young clerk-typist named Angelina, who had just been assigned to the station to help catch up on a records backlog. At first, he had been amused by the obvious mistake concerning his whereabouts. Here he was standing around drinking coffee and being relentlessly witty and cute for the new personnel, and these people thought he was off on some kind of expedition with an archaeo-astronomy professor his father had worked for when Toomey was a boy.

Very funny.

Except that the professor wasn't a practical joke kind of woman, and after a moment or two, he remembered that. She was precise, exacting and no-nonsense. Her long interest in the Anasazi ruins had been in the Old Ones' use of astronomy and their possible observatories, rather than their trash heaps and potsherds. She had wanted to know how they marked time and the summer and winter solstices. He'd once seen her uncover the mathematical precision of a ruined building by the positions of its seemingly random tiny windows. He'd seen her locate nearly the exact center of a ruin simply by snapping her fingers and listening to the echoes. She had that kind of mind, the kind that wouldn't do anything so out of character as to pointedly mention a certain Navajo police officer and then disappear.

Crazy, he thought again.

He walked back to the police utility vehicle to call in to the dispatcher. He had made a point of giving his position as exactly as he could all along the way. It was the only thing he could think of that might temper Lieutenant Singer's anticipated aggravation with him. Regardless of the fact that he was the logical person to come out here, Toomey hadn't waited to be officially assigned. He had taken matters into his own hands, because Lucas Singer had been out of the building and unavailable when the call came in. It was not a wise decision for anyone as far down in the pecking order as Toomey was. And the lieutenant wouldn't cut him any slack, because Toomey had been entirely too helpful in getting Captain Johnny Becenti—whose job it was to tell *both* of them what to do—married to Lucas's sister, Lillian. It was Toomey's understanding—*now*—that Becenti and Lucas Singer had barely tolerated each other for years—which explained why Lucas was still somewhat less than thrilled with the marriage and the junior officer who had done his part to bring it about.

Toomey sighed. Well, perhaps he hadn't done all that much. Mostly, he'd just kept his mouth shut about what he knew and when he knew it. It had nearly killed him not to tell anyone—a couple as unlikely and mismatched as Becenti and Lucas's too-good-for-the-rez lawyer sister was big news. In fact, the People were still talking about it. But Toomey had managed to stay silent, even under the onslaught of questions from longtime tribal police dispatcher and resident busybody, Mary Skeets. And he had learned a thing or two in the process. How to stand up under Mary Skeets's intense interrogation, for one thing, and how totally unpredictable male-female relationships could be, for another. It didn't seem to matter how indifferent and unreceptive a man thought he was to becoming involved with a particular woman. If she was the *right* woman, she could still turn him completely around. The problem was whether or not the man could survive the turning.

Toomey sighed again. He had decided all the things he would tell the lieutenant about his one-man quest to locate Edna Trevoy, but there was one thing he wouldn't tell him. He wouldn't say how uneasy all this business with Dr. Trevoy had made him. He was still uneasy, out of harmony, caught knee-deep in something that was not in keeping with the usual chaos of his life and something that he didn't begin to understand. He didn't like surprises, and he was increasingly certain he was about to get one.

He waited what seemed a long time for the dispatcher to respond. He kept hoping that he hadn't gotten into one of those ever-changing pockets of interference that wreaked havoc with radio communications on the rez.

The dispatcher—Mary Skeets—finally answered him. The professor was still lost, she said—unless *he* had found her. Her tone of voice suggested that his current situation would be much improved if he had.

"No, Mary," he said. "I think I've located the entrance into the arroyo, but I can't be absolutely sure in the dark. I'm going to wait until the others get here before I go in. Does the lieutenant want to talk to me?"

"Oh, yeah," she assured him, and it was clear to him that he might as well accept the fact that he was always going to be in trouble with Lucas Singer. And it wasn't that Toomey did it deliberately—well, today he had done it deliberately, but there were mitigating circumstances.

"Okay," he said. "Put him on."

"My information is that the lieutenant is on his way out to where you are," Mary advised him, and he closed his eyes and swore. Being lectured via the radio and having half the tribal police force hear it was one thing. Facing Lucas Singer in person was something else again.

"Okay," he said again, because there was a chance Lucas was hearing the transmission even now—but he didn't mean it. He signed off and got out of the utility vehicle, looking back down the dirt track in the direction he had come for headlights. He didn't see anything yet.

What if this isn't the way in?

The thought presented itself with great authority and led to a host of other notions that were equally unsettling. What if the lieutenant couldn't find him. What if the lieutenant *did* find him? He had no idea which would be worse. What if he'd gone off by himself like this, dragged Lucas Singer all the way out here, and it wasn't the right place? If so, he was pretty sure he could kiss town life goodbye. The lieutenant would have him shipped off to some tribal police outpost so fast he wouldn't know what hit him. It would be months before he'd be able to have any kind of social life again. No flirting with Angelina around the coffeepot, no hope of taking her out dancing, no nothing.

He checked his flashlight to make sure it was still working, then walked back to the slit in the rocks. If Edna Trevoy had gone in there, then why? It was true that the two of them were likely the only people who knew that the wall with the petroglyphs existed; she'd called it her "ace in the hole" and sworn him to secrecy. He had happened upon it when his father was working as a guide and gofer for her. Young Ben Toomey had been allowed to come along on this particular trek because he was interested in the search for ruined watchtowers and faded glyphs and because he knew how to stay out of the way and not cause trouble—a trait he earnestly wished had followed him into his adulthood. Even so, he had been a boy with time on his hands that day, and he had gone into the slit between the huge rocks simply because it was there and he could. He had realized immediately that there was more to the place than first met the eye. He had kept going, following the narrow, winding path, knowing instinctively that he was perhaps the first human to do so in nearly a thousand years.

He finally came out at the big overhang with the decorated rock wall beneath it. The pictograph was clearly visible. Four spirals and a handprint. And some kind of mark above them he couldn't recognize. The professor was particularly interested in spirals, and he knew she would be interested in this. It had taken some doing to tell her about it, because she had been more than a little annoyed by his abrupt disappearance.

Eventually, she had listened long enough to understand that he had found something for her, and she had let him lead her in. Incredibly, she had wept at the sight of it. She kept moving from glyph to glyph, wiping her eyes on her shirtsleeve, so overcome with emotion that she would have actually placed her hand exactly on the ancient handprint if he hadn't stopped her. He had believed in the evil that came from the dead then, and he'd tried to protect her from it, surprising himself and her with his audacity. But she had seemed...touched, he supposed was the word. She hadn't laughed at him or tried to persuade him of the ridiculousness of his primitive beliefs. Actually, what she had done that day, he suddenly realized, was make a friend for life, so much so that he was braving Lucas Singer's wrath to come see about her.

Toomey had always understood what a complex woman Edna Trevoy was. She was brash and yet gentle. She chain-smoked, yet constantly reiterated what she would personally do to him if he ever took up the habit. Comparatively speaking, she was light-years away from the Angelinas of the world. The Angelinas only needed to be admired and to have somebody to flirt with, preferably to the accompaniment of loud music on a smoky dance floor. The Edna Trevoys needed to be surrounded by a host of naysayers while they attempted the impossible. And this one had spent most of her life developing her own avant-garde theories to decipher a lost people.

She was totally obsessed with finding some kind of purpose to their lives, and yet at one point she had dropped everything to have a child. If she had ever had a husband, Toomey hadn't heard about it—at least the husband didn't hang around the archaeological digs with her and her name had never changed. Toomey remembered the little dark-haired girl who was Edna's daughter, remembered that he had showed off for her on occasion—until his father would notice and find him something more productive to expend his energy on. She had been a year or so younger than he, and for a time she had trailed in her mother's footsteps from one archaeological site to another around the rez. As he recalled, when she was old enough, she had been abruptly packed off to an Eastern boarding school. He remembered his own mother's empathy for the professor at the time, because she, too, had had to send her children away to a school. Toomey doubted that his mother had

ever grasped that what had been forced upon her by the
Bureau of Indian Affairs, Edna Trevoy had likely em-
braced willingly. He wondered idly what had happened to
Edna's daughter. Married by now, maybe, or like her
mother, obsessed by a career.

It was cold with the sun gone down, and the wind had
picked up. He kept looking for headlights in the distance,
listening for the sound of a vehicle approaching. A coyote
barked not far away, and yet another one answered. He
looked skyward. Not much of a moon tonight. Maybe he
should backtrack and find the lieutenant, he thought. How
much hell he would catch was likely directly proportional
to how easy he was to find.

He turned his head sharply at a small sound that was
taken by the wind before he could identify it. He walked
closer to the slit, thinking it had come from that direction.

Nothing. No sound. No movement.

He stood there, his anxiety rising.

What if she's hurt? he thought.

He was already in trouble. He didn't think he could
make it much worse by going ahead and looking for her.
The woman was older than his mother. She could have
fallen, broken something, and if she had, time was of the
essence.

Something suddenly occurred to him, and he walked
back to the utility vehicle. He would tell the lieutenant
where he was going—but not via the radio. He wasn't
going to chance having Lucas order him to stay put. He
climbed in and started the engine, then backed it around
so that it faced the huge rocks. He turned on the headlights,
then backed up a few more feet so that they shone directly
on the slit.

Okay, he thought. Good enough.

He took the notepad he had in his shirt pocket and wrote

quickly: "Turn on the headlights. The place between the two big rocks—where the lights hit—is where I've gone. Toomey."

He got out of the vehicle and closed the piece of paper in the door, tugging on it to make sure it would stay and that it was clearly visible. Then he walked back to the entrance. There was no point in waiting any longer. It would be better if he verified the situation before the lieutenant arrived.

Yes, Dr. Trevoy is in there, or no, she's not.

He zipped up his jacket because he was cold and because he didn't want it catching on anything when he tried to get through. He walked back to the entrance and he stood for a moment, shining his flashlight into the crevice. He wasn't afraid, just...uneasy.

He worked his way in between the rocks, moving sideways. After a short distance, there wasn't a wide enough space for him to put his feet all the way down flat, and his knees scraped along the rock with every step. But he kept going, shining his flashlight from time to time to make sure the way was clear. He couldn't hear anything—except his own labored breathing as he struggled to get through. He was having to try to stay up on the sides of the rocks themselves now, because he had run out of path. He didn't remember having to do this before, but it didn't overly concern him. As a boy he would have been perfectly happy to climb along the face of a rock instead of walk on the ground, but he was twenty-five now.

The path reappeared, and he stepped onto it, but there was also an abrupt downward slope, causing him to lose his balance and hit his head hard on the horizontal trunk of a small tree growing out of the rock. He had thought that he was in good physical shape, but he was completely out of breath by the time he emerged on the other side.

His forehead throbbed from the collision with the tree, and he leaned against the huge boulder for a moment to recover. There was a strong updraft here, a sustained sigh in the wind he could almost but not quite hear. He realized suddenly that he could smell wood smoke.

Encouraged, he walked on, moving carefully in the dark. The smell of smoke grew stronger, and something else. Coffee?

He kept going, quietly rounding a boulder. He could see the glow of the fire now.

"Stop where you are," a woman's voice said, making him jump. She was standing off to his right in the shadows. He couldn't see her, couldn't tell anything about her, except that the voice was not Edna Trevoy's and that she didn't seem to mind that he turned his flashlight in her general direction. "Who are you?" she asked.

"Officer Ben Toomey," he said. "Navajo Tribal Police."

She didn't say anything; there was only a slight sound. Was she laughing? He couldn't tell that, either, without putting the light directly on her. But if she was, he failed to see the humor here.

"I'm sorry," she said. "I didn't mean to scare you—"

"You didn't," he said, his male pride making him lie. "Who are you?"

She didn't quite answer the question. "You're looking for my mother, I guess. She said you'd come. She's over here."

She stepped out onto the path then, and when he didn't immediately follow her, she turned back to him.

"Well, come on," she said. "She's waiting."

This is crazy, he thought yet another time. This young woman—Edna's daughter—was behaving as if he were unfashionably late for afternoon tea.

He could see the campfire now, a small one near the overhang that protected the wall with the petroglyphs. And it was coffee he had smelled.

"Wait," he said, hoping to make her turn around again so he could see if she was indeed the daughter he remembered. "What are you doing out here?"

"I don't exactly know," she said, glancing back at him over her shoulder. "I was hoping maybe you could find out."

She continued on, and there was nothing for him to do but follow. Edna Trevoy sat leaning against a rock, her legs inside a sleeping bag. The daughter knelt down beside her.

"Mother?" she said. "Mother?"

Edna Trevoy stirred immediately.

"He's here. Ben Toomey is here."

"Benjamin," Edna said, holding out her hand in his direction. "I knew you'd come. I knew you'd understand."

"Well, I wouldn't go that far," Toomey said, coming closer and squatting down beside her. He took her hand in his. Her fingers were cold and frail—much more frail than he remembered. "Miss Edna," he said kindly. "What the hell are you doing out here?"

She laughed softly and squeezed his hand before she let go. "Tying up loose ends, Benjamin. You want some coffee?"

"No, I want to know what you're doing out here. How did you get here? You know half the tribal police force is out looking for you."

"Are they?" she said, clearly unimpressed. "I didn't expect that. The plan was just for you to come." She gave a sigh. "Well—no matter. You're here, and that's what counts."

"Miss Edna—"

"Drink some coffee, Benjamin. So I won't feel so guilty about dragging you out here. You still like it, don't you? I remember that you did when you were a little boy. You used to sneak it when you thought nobody was looking."

He glanced at Edna's daughter, but he wasn't getting any help from her. Clearly, she was as literally and figuratively in the dark as he was.

"Well," he said. "What we need to do now is get you out of here—"

"No!" Edna said, clutching at his arm. "Not yet. It's not the twenty-first."

"The twenty-first?"

"Tomorrow—after the sun comes up, I'll leave. But not now, Benjamin. I won't go now."

"Miss Edna, it's cold out here. You're going to make yourself sick—"

"Oh, my dear boy, that is no longer a consideration. I just need a little time—until after sunrise. And I need both of you here. Is that too much to ask? I haven't broken any laws."

He wasn't sure about that. Making people think she had disappeared and falsely involving the tribal police must at least bend one or two.

Still, it would be hard to prove.

"Get yourself some coffee," she said, back to that again. "I'm tired. I'm going to rest now so I'll be ready for the morning. We'll talk some more later. I have something important I want to ask you."

"Miss Edna—"

"I'm very tired, Benjamin," she said, her voice as frail now as her hands had been. She slid down into the sleeping bag and turned onto her side, facing away from him.

Toomey waited for a few minutes, then stood up. Edna's

daughter was quietly putting some dead wood on the fire. She had her hair cut in one of those artfully disheveled, but very chic styles that his youngest, "still in beauty school" sister was always trying to perfect. She was forever looking for a head to practice on. He considered himself very lucky indeed that she hadn't yet tried to cut his hair like *that*. Edna's daughter's hair hung in her face—just the way it was supposed to, and her profile—what he could see of it—was edged in firelight. Even under these poorly illuminated conditions, he could tell that she had the "look," the one that said she had always had the best of everything. The right schools, the right clothes, the right fork for the right cuisine. He had first learned about her kind when he was in college. She was one of the rich girls who had passed through his academic life, expensive rose-colored glasses firmly in place, never noticing that he, and all the other "here on a scholarship" misfits like him, even existed.

Pretty, anyway, he thought. But if his memory served him correctly, he had thought she was pretty enough to show off for when she was barely nine. Now if he could just remember her white name. He wasn't sure that he'd ever known it. He only knew the name that his father and the rest of Edna's Navajo workers had given her as a child—Follows-like-a-Lamb, because she was always so diligent about keeping up with her mother's whereabouts on those long ago searches in the Anasazi ruins. Toomey wondered then as he did now if it was because she was afraid or because she was obedient. She must be obedient, he decided, or she wouldn't be out here in this desolate place tonight.

He waited for her to stand up. She was taller than he'd first thought, but he still looked down on her, a fact that pleased him for some reason. "I have to go—" he started to say.

"No, please don't," she interrupted, and she was clearly alarmed by the prospect. "Can't you stay until the sun comes up? Please."

"I'm going to try to do that," he said, "but I have to radio in. I have to let my superiors know I've found your mother."

"You aren't going to try to make her leave, are you?"

"I...don't see any reason to do that right now. Did she say anything to you at all about why she wanted to come out here?"

"Just what she told you. She's tying up loose ends." She gave a wavering sigh. "She's been sick. And I think she's ignoring whatever it is that's wrong with her. I think maybe it's gotten worse—but she won't *say*. She won't tell me anything. I don't even know if she's seen a doctor. I hadn't heard from her for weeks—I wasn't even sure where she was. And then all of a sudden I have to drop everything and come way out here—" She stopped abruptly. "I'm sorry. I didn't mean that the way it sounded. I'd do anything for my mother. It's just that I'm so worried."

"I understand," he said. "You...think her mind is clear." It wasn't quite a question.

"This craziness aside, as far as I can tell she's our usual hardheaded Edna."

He smiled briefly and turned to go.

"You'll come back?" she asked, obviously still worried.

"Yes. As soon as I can."

"Ben," she said.

He looked back at her.

"Thank you," she said.

Don't thank me yet, he thought. He had no idea what the lieutenant would have to say about all this. If he had arrived, then Toomey would just have to tell him everything he knew—which he realized was precious little. Edna Trevoy was found, at least, and he earnestly hoped that would satisfy Lucas Singer.

There was no one around when he emerged from the rocks. When he shone his flashlight, he could see the piece of paper still stuck in the utility vehicle door. Clearly, the lieutenant hadn't found his location. He walked out to the vehicle. He could hear the radio—Mary Skeets trying to get him to respond—well before he reached it.

"There you are," she said pleasantly when he answered, but another voice immediately cut in.

"Toomey, where the hell have you been!"

The transmission was punctuated with static, but Toomey had no trouble recognizing the voice. It wasn't Lucas. It was Captain Becenti, and he realized immediately that he'd allowed himself to become yet another reason for Lieutenant Singer and Captain Becenti to annoy each other. He toyed briefly with the idea of pretending that he couldn't copy anything Becenti said.

"I, ah, found Dr. Trevoy, sir," he said instead, deciding to get to the bottom line before Becenti could ask. "She's all right. She's in the arroyo."

"Doing what?" Becenti wanted to know.

"Tying up loose ends, she says."

"Am I supposed to understand that?"

"No, sir. I don't understand myself. She says she's staying until sunrise tomorrow. She's got her daughter with her."

"Why was she letting people think she was going in there with you?"

"Don't know, sir. I thought I'd stay here and try to find out—if that's okay."

Becenti didn't answer. Toomey waited. The silence lengthened. He was prepared to go into more detail; he was even prepared to ask for a vacation day—if he had to.

"You're sure Dr. Trevoy is all right," Becenti said finally.

"As far as I can tell. She's not hurt or anything. She's just acting a little strange. Her daughter's kind of worried about her. Dr. Trevoy has always been on the high side of eccentric—but I wouldn't want to go off and leave the two of them alone out here. I'm not even sure how they got here—there's no vehicle."

"You see me first thing when you get back," Becenti said. "You make sure those people are safe and you see me tomorrow morning, understand? Without fail."

"Yes, sir," Toomey assured him, but he quietly breathed a sigh of relief. There was nothing like delaying the inevitable to raise a man's spirits.

He fished out the blanket he kept in the vehicle, and then he sat there for a moment, gathering his thoughts. So far so good with this thing—except that he had no idea what was going on and he still couldn't think of the daughter's given name.

She was sitting near the fire when he returned, and she looked up sharply when he approached. He could see her face well enough to realize that she hadn't believed him when he said he would come back.

"Are you staying?" she asked immediately.

"Yes," he said. "But I have to leave in the morning. And you and Dr. Trevoy will have to come with me."

"No problem," she said. "This place—" She shook her head. "There's absolutely nobody here but us, and I still feel so...crowded, you know? Like I'm going to back into somebody or step on their feet if I'm not careful."

He knew exactly. "That feeling is the reason my people—if they've got a choice—stay away from these places."

"But your father worked the digs."

"*Choice,* is the key word here. He had five children to feed."

She didn't say anything else, and he looked in Dr. Trevoy's direction. She appeared to be sleeping. He stood awkwardly for a moment, then walked to the fire. Surprisingly, Edna's daughter came with him.

"If you want coffee, I'll get you some," she said.

"I can do it," he said, putting the blanket roll down. He took the enamel splatterware cup and the small ragged pot holder she offered him and carefully poured the coffee from the pot, savoring the aroma. Edna Trevoy had been right. He had loved coffee as a boy, and he still did. After a moment, he tentatively tasted it.

Not bad, he thought, but then Miss Edna had had years of practice at brewing coffee on a campfire. He moved to sit on a nearby boulder to drink it, and he completely discarded the possibility that her daughter might have made it. He kept looking at her. She was very busy now, putting on the earphones to her CD player, he assumed, so she could better ignore him.

"So what are you listening to?" he asked after a moment, because he saw no point in making it easy. She surprised him by coming closer and handing him the earphones. He sat his cup down and put them on—some kind of alternative rock, a piano, and a yodeling and plaintive female soprano voice, agonizing about winter and something—someone—lost forever.

"What is it?" he asked after a moment.

She fought down a smile.

"I'm glad you find my ignorance so amusing," he said. He handed back the earphones. To his surprise, Edna's daughter didn't go away. She sat down on the ground close to him.

"No—no, it's not that," she said. "It's the name of the song. It's called 'Ben's Song.'"

"Yeah? Catchy."

"Well, actually, I think it's some kind of funeral dirge."

"Funeral dirge," he repeated. He looked around him. "Just what you ought to be listening to out here."

"My mother says you went to the University of New Mexico," she said after a moment.

"Yes," he said.

"In Albuquerque."

"Yes," he said again, still feeling awkward now and wondering what else Dr. Trevoy had said about him. And why. He picked up his cup and sipped the coffee, and he told her when he'd been at the university.

"I was there most of that time. Maybe we had some classes together."

"We didn't," he said bluntly.

She looked at him, but she made no comment.

"Most of my classes had alphabetical seating," he said, feeling the need to explain. "'Toomey' would have been close to 'Trevoy.' If you'd been there, I would have remembered."

She didn't make any reply to that, either, and they sat for a time in silence. He wished she would say something. She had a soft and pleasant voice. He wondered how much of it had been learned. People—women—he knew didn't sound the way she did. He could just smell the perfume she wore—or maybe it wasn't perfume. Maybe it was simply her. It was very delicate. And pleasant. Like the voice.

He looked up at the sky for something to do.

"Officer Toomey, are—" she began.

"Ben," he interrupted, an act of rudeness on his part that would have definitely given his mother and grandmothers and several aunts pause. He'd had an abundance of relatives to teach him how to behave, but at this particular moment he was more interested in why she had suddenly decided to be so formal.

He waited for her to continue. She didn't. He could feel her looking at him.

"I don't know your name," he said after a time.

"Trevoy," she said pointedly, and he laughed.

"No, your given name. I remember your Navajo name, but not your..." He was going to say "white name," but he thought better of it.

"My Navajo name? I don't have a Navajo name."

"Actually, you do. My father and the rest of the men who worked for your mother gave it to you." He said it for her in Navajo.

"What does it mean?"

He told her that, too, and he could almost, but not quite, see her frown.

"When it comes to naming things, we're a literal people," he said, because he thought that she found the translation unsettling. "It wasn't intended as an insult or a criticism or anything like that. It was just the way you were then—always following—like a lamb."

"I was scared," she said, answering the question he'd had earlier. "You know what my mother is like. Hanging on to Edna was a full-time job for a little kid. I never knew when she was going to just up and leave for weeks at a time. It was a little better when I got old enough to come along—but not much. And I was always afraid of that room."

"What room?"

"The room they found in one of the ruins. The one with the man and his thirteen concubines—or whatever they were—buried in it. All the women had been executed."

"Oh, *that* room," he said, and he could feel her smile.

"I figured if there was one such place, there must be a thousand. And small female children ought not be hanging around them."

"Very sensible," he said.

"Maybe to you, but not to Edna. She sent me to boarding school when I was eight. It was a relief actually—to be someplace where the adults stayed put. After a while, I got to the point where I could even sleep all night and not worry that everybody would be gone in the morning."

"I'm sorry," he said, certain now of what he'd always suspected. That Edna's daughter may have had the best "things," but that her childhood had been a lot worse than his.

"No, I'm sorry," she said. "I shouldn't be telling you all this. It certainly doesn't matter at this late date. It's just the way it was. Little kids learn to adjust."

The conversation lagged again.

"You didn't tell me your given name," he said after a time.

"Eden," she said. "It was either that or Irmangarde."

"Irmangarde?" he said, chuckling.

"I swear. That was one of Edna's choices. Don't ask me why. I think she toyed with the idea of naming me after her, too, but she couldn't quite make herself do it. 'Eden' was as close as she could get. Too confusing for the archaeological community if I happened to follow in her footsteps. How would people know which Edna wrote the paper?"

There it was again. That slight edge to her voice he'd

heard earlier when she spoke of her mother. Maybe she would do anything for Edna Trevoy, and she may have adjusted to having been left behind and then sent away to a private school—but she hadn't forgiven her for it.

"You look like an 'Eden,'" he said.

"Oh, good," she said. "That's a relief. I thought you were going to say I looked like a lamb."

He laughed again. He was enjoying this. He was *really* enjoying this.

"Is that blanket going to be enough?" she asked.

"Yes," he said, his mind indulging in a brief fantasy as to what she might suggest if it wasn't. "I'll be fine."

"Okay, then," she said. "I think I'll go to sleep, too. I've got my watch alarm set, but if it shouldn't work or something, would you make sure my mother is awake before the sun comes up? She's worried about that—about missing the sunrise."

"Can do," he said.

He finished his coffee and he was careful not to watch as she got into her sleeping bag. As much as he wanted to, it would have been impolite to stare, and he had ignored his upbringing enough for one night.

He unrolled his blanket and wrapped it around him, expecting to half doze the rest of the night the way he always did when he was on stakeout. The only problem was that he felt more restless than sleepy. He wasn't happy just sitting there. He was still out of harmony, and this place did nothing to restore it.

But he must have slept after all, because he opened his eyes suddenly, not knowing for a moment where he was. Both women were still in their sleeping bags. He looked up at the night sky. The constellations were no longer where he had last seen them. So much for the trained and ever-alert police officer, he thought, and he smiled to himself. Big college graduate or not, no one would have any trouble telling he was traditional and hogan raised. He had looked at the sky first, and then at his watch.

The fire had burned down to embers, and he came out of his blanket to put some more wood on. He wasn't the least bit sleepy now, and after a moment he took out his flashlight and walked to the glyphs. They were pretty much the way he remembered. The rocky overhang had protected them for a thousand years and would for a thousand more. Spirals. A handprint. A symbol he hadn't recognized when he was a boy, but did now. The Pueblo Twins, born of a maiden who had been imprisoned in a tower. Her only visitor had been the Sun. One day she lay down in front of her tower window, and the Sun impregnated her. The result was the boy twins, who protected her people.

But not very well, he thought, because her people had vanished.

"Beautiful, isn't it?" Dr. Trevoy said at his elbow.

"Enduring, anyway," he said, glancing at her. She was very agile for her age and for her frailness and her claim of fatigue. He hadn't heard her approach. "Feeling better?"

"Much better," she said. "You know what this is, don't you?"

"I know what this glyph is here," he said, shining the flashlight on the Pueblo Twins. "But I have no idea what the whole thing is." He had determined since his Native American studies at UNM, that archaeologists and anthropologists sometimes took these things far too seriously. He knew from some of the interpretations of his own culture how far off they could be sometimes—and his were a living people. There were all kinds of guesses among the academic types as to what the spirals meant. And the handprints. He thought it as likely that some long-lost Anasazi got up one day and simply felt like decorating a rock wall as anything else. But Dr. Trevoy and her kind had an ability to take something seemingly random and insignificant and draw some profound conclusions. He didn't. He relied more on the feelings a place evoked, and for that reason—simple decorations or not—he was uneasy here just as he had been when he was a boy.

"It's a calendar, Benjamin," Dr. Trevoy said. "At least I think it is. And at sunrise today—June the twenty-first—I'll know for certain."

He waited, giving her the opportunity to say whatever else she had to say. But she kept looking at the glyphs and then up at the sky to gauge how long she had until the sun came up.

"When are you going to get around to telling me what all this is really about, Miss Edna?" he asked quietly when he thought he'd waited long enough.

She looked at him sharply, and then at her sleeping daughter.

"There's more to it than your needing to verify a calendar on the day of the summer solstice," he said.

She sighed.

"Yes, you're right, Benjamin—but, of course, you really should be here today. You're the one who found it."

"You know you've caused me trouble with my boss," he went on. He wanted her to understand that whatever this little game of hers was, it had its consequences.

"Oh," she said. "I didn't think of that, either, Benjamin. I just wanted you to be here—for the sunrise. And for the other thing."

"What other thing?"

"You're the only one I could ask," she said, evading the question. "I know you, you see. And your father and mother. I know how well you were brought up, and that you've studied your people. I always kept up with you when you were at the university. You didn't know that, did you?''

"Miss Edna—''

"I might have asked your father to do it—if he'd lived, because he was an honorable man, and my friend, I think. I believe he would have done his best for me."

Toomey took a quiet breath. His father and his uncles had gone out of their way to teach him the virtue of patience—but his was wearing thin at the moment.

"Are you going to tell me what it is you want me to do?" he asked.

She smiled. "You are such a *policeman,* Benjamin. Persistent in getting at the truth. Firm, but polite. I'm impressed." Her smile faded. "It may be that you won't have to do anything at all," she said. "That will be up to Eden. Would you leave me alone here for just a little while? Go back to sleep if you want—"

"Miss Edna—"

She held up her hand. "Please, Benjamin. All will be revealed—or almost all. I've rested, and now I need just a little time to prepare mentally. This is very difficult for me, you understand."

No, he didn't understand. That was the problem. But he left her and walked back to the fire. He wrapped himself in his blanket again and sat down. And it only took him a moment to realize that Eden Trevoy wasn't asleep. He could feel her wakefulness. He could hear...

He turned his head in her direction. He couldn't see her face, but he was sure now. Eden Trevoy, the rich girl who had everything, was crying.

Chapter Two

Eden realized that Officer Ben Toomey wasn't at all good at pretending—either that he hadn't heard her crying when he had or that this situation was somehow nothing out of the ordinary when it obviously was. She did appreciate, however, the fact that he seemed to be making some effort to be discreet. He wouldn't quite meet her eyes if she happened to be looking at him. But when he thought she wasn't, he stared. She could literally feel him trying to understand what was happening here. Little did he know how impossible that was. She had spent her entire life trying to fathom Edna Trevoy—and she had never even gotten a hint as to what her mother was about.

Eden hadn't meant to cry—and she certainly hadn't meant for Ben Toomey to hear her. It was the lack of sleep and the worry that had caused her emotions to come so close to the surface. She was so *tired,* and everything had come unraveled suddenly, all those years of trying to get her relationship with her mother into the proper perspective, of trying to accept once and for all that Edna Trevoy was a dry well and that one could go to that well a thousand times and still come back with absolutely nothing. Suddenly the old sense of loss and abandonment had overwhelmed her. It was as if she were eight years old again and packed off to boarding school. She was in a situation she didn't begin to understand, any more than Toomey did, one that bespoke of losing her tenuous grasp on her mother's love and affection yet another time.

I am not *going to do this!* she thought abruptly, slamming her backpack aside with enough force to cause both Toomey and her mother to look around. I'm not a little kid. I have a job—no, I have a *career.* I make my own money. I have my own life. I can whine and make myself feel bad because Edna wasn't Mother-of-the-Year or I can get on with it.

She stood up and walked purposefully to the place where Toomey and Edna stood, not saying anything to either of them. She had agreed to help with this latest project, and she would keep her word. She checked the expensive video camera one last time and placed it on the tripod. She had filmed the shaft of sunlight on the petroglyphs on the previous two mornings. This morning was supposed to be *it*—whatever *it* was. In any event, she would record the event, and that would be that. Then she would get out of here and back to her life in Albuquerque—until the next time Edna deigned to summon her.

She looked at her watch and then up at what sky she could see between the tall boulders.

"It won't be long now," her mother said, and Eden nodded.

Not long. And then what?

"You'll remember to take photographs, too?" Edna insisted.

"Yes, Mother. Everything's ready. I won't miss a thing. I'll even take a picture of handsome Officer Toomey here, if you want."

"What a fine idea!" Edna enthused, making Toomey smile. He had a rather nice smile, Eden thought—a little shy and therefore at odds with his resolute police officer persona, but he was absolutely aware that the Trevoy women were shamelessly teasing him.

"You'd do better to watch the sun," he said. "It's not going to shine into this narrow space very long. You don't want to miss anything."

"Heaven forbid," Edna said. "Where's my stool?"

Toomey got it for her and placed it where she wanted it—several times.

"Perfect," she said finally. "Thank you, my dear Benjamin."

"You're welcome, Miss Edna," he answered, glancing at Eden. The look held.

Eden appreciated the rapport Toomey and her mother seemed to have; it appeared to be far beyond anything she'd ever been able to establish with Edna. Her mother had chosen her knight errant—or whatever Toomey was supposed to be—well. And he *had* heard Eden crying. If she had had any doubts before, she had none now. The compassion she saw in his eyes was such that she came close to crying all over again.

She gave a sharp sigh and began to fiddle with the camera hanging around her neck. She wasn't used to this. Heretofore, she'd hardly acknowledged even to herself that she wanted—needed—empathy and understanding from another human being. It was completely foreign to her, completely unsettling. And it wasn't embarrassment she felt now so much as dismay. She didn't even know Ben Toomey, and here he was, somehow privy to a pain that was so personal and so private that even she rarely allowed herself to recognize it.

"Here we go," Edna said suddenly. "Eden, are you ready? Is the videotape going?"

"Everything's working, Mother," she said, getting back to the job at hand.

She began to snap pictures of the two small shafts of light that had entered the row of petroglyphs from either end—and several of the unsuspecting Toomey.

Actually he was rather handsome, she decided, moving to get a better shot.

"What exactly are we supposed to see?" he asked, looking in her direction when she was about to attempt yet another angle of him. She immediately went back to shooting the glyphs.

"You've heard of the 'sun dagger'?" Edna said.

"Vaguely, yes," he said.

"Well, this isn't it. *This,* I believe, is the 'sun serpent,' the actual manifestation of the one found on so much of the pottery."

"And?"

"And it's going to bisect the spirals dead center—all the way across. By doing so, it's going to show us—and all the Anasazi ghosts I'm sure have gathered about—that today is indeed the summer solstice—time for planting, time for—"

Edna abruptly stopped talking as opposing shafts of light cut the first and last spirals in two.

"The video camera—it's working, Eden?" she asked urgently.

"It's working," Eden said.

"Take pictures!"

"Yes, Mother, I am," she said patiently.

"Look!" Edna said. "It is! Oh, it *is!*"

The shaft of light continued from both directions across the face of the rock, undulating like the sun serpent it was supposed to represent, bisecting each of the spirals until it finally joined into a single zigzag ribbon of sunlight through the center of all the glyphs.

"The sun didn't do this yesterday?" Toomey said at Eden's elbow.

"No," Eden answered, still snapping away. "She's right about it hitting the spirals dead center on the twenty-first of June—but who knows if it means anything."

"It means something," he said. "To her."

"Look, Eden—Benjamin, look!" Edna cried, her hands clasped together at her throat. "Professors Stepp and Hill are going to absolutely—"

"Mother!" Eden interrupted, knowing that Edna was about to cut loose with one of her colorful metaphors. "A little decorum here—remember Toomey's virgin ears."

"Benjamin has heard worse than that from me," Edna assured her.

"Then it's a wonder he came out here."

"No, actually, the wonder is that I could find this place again," he said, smiling tolerantly as they continued to plague him with their teasing.

"Well, I, for one, am very glad you did," Edna said. "You shouldn't have missed this. This is *your* find."

"Only because I was sticking my nose where it shouldn't have been."

"Ah, but, Benjamin, nearly all great discoveries are made just so," Edna said. "Now. I believe we've seen all there is to see here. Shall we pack up?"

"You're sure?" Eden asked, because she'd known her

mother to completely change her mind about whether or not everything had been seen on more than one occasion.

"Perfectly," Edna said. She stood up from her camp stool, only to immediately sit down again with enough force to alarm Toomey.

"Wait," Eden whispered to him. She was close enough to him to put her hand on his arm to keep him from going to her mother's aid, and she did so. "Wait," she whispered again. "She doesn't want help. Believe me."

After a moment Edna stood up again, this time with more success. She waited for a moment, then walked unsteadily to the place where her sleeping bag and backpack lay.

"What's wrong with her?" Toomey asked.

"I told you. She won't say."

"You did ask?"

"Of course, I *asked*. A hundred times. All I can get out of her is some kind of fractured platitude—like 'The milk has already hit the floor, Eden,' or 'The barn door is off its hinges, Eden.' Period."

Their eyes met, and Eden looked abruptly away. What she had interpreted as compassion earlier, she now recognized for what it actually was. Pity. Ben Toomey felt sorry for her.

She abruptly moved past him to begin packing up the video equipment. He didn't offer to help—incredibly astute of him, she thought. She didn't want his help or anyone else's.

"Benjamin," her mother called to him, and he walked in Edna's direction, only to be sent back again to fetch her stool.

But this time she wasn't nearly so particular about where he placed it. She sat down immediately. Eden could hear them talking, and she realized after a moment that her mother was speaking Navajo. When in the world had Edna become conversant in the Navajo language? she wondered. She had never mentioned that she was learning, and that was one of the very few things Edna would have been expected to share. Her mother had worked for years with her hired Navajo guides and diggers, and Eden had never heard her make any attempt to speak anything but English to them. So where did this come from? Surely Edna wasn't making a career change to linguistics at this late date.

The conversation continued. And either Toomey didn't understand at all or he understood and disagreed. Whatever Edna's question was, his answer was categorically *N'dah.* No.

Toomey abruptly walked away a few steps and then came back again. This time he sat down on the ground so that he was no longer towering over her, his manner resigned: *Tell me. I'm listening.*

Edna Trevoy told him. And told him. He kept shaking his head. Eden thought he was going to get up and walk away again. But finally—finally—her mother convinced him—or made him understand—or whatever she was doing—because she was Dr. Edna Trevoy, and few could withstand her iron will. Incredibly, as Eden watched, her mother removed an envelope from her jacket pocket and held it out to him. He didn't take it. Edna insisted—no, pleaded.

Edna Trevoy was pleading?

Eden stopped pretending that she was occupied with packing up the equipment and blatantly watched. Toomey still hesitated, then finally took the envelope and shoved it into his breast pocket.

What was it? Money? Edna was paying him for something?

He abruptly stood up again and walked away, hesitating

long enough to pick up his blanket, and this time he didn't come back to Edna for more discussion. He kept going, up the rocky path and into the stone crevice that led out of the arroyo, without once looking back.

"What have you done now, Mother?" Eden asked bluntly.

"Done?" Edna said, starting as if she'd forgotten that Eden was here.

"Yes, 'done.' To Toomey. He's upset. Why?"

"He's not upset."

"Oh, yes, he is. Benjamin Toomey is someone who should never play poker. Where is he going?"

Edna sighed heavily. "He's gone out to wait."

"For what?"

"For us."

"For—I *knew* you'd change your mind. Now what are we going to do?"

"We're going to talk."

"Talk," Eden repeated, not at all certain she'd heard right.

"Yes," Edna said pointedly. "Talk. I say something and then you say something—back and forth until the topic is exhausted."

"Well, it's an interesting idea, but I don't think it'll ever work. Especially where you and I are concerned." She began to roll up Edna's sleeping bag.

"Eden," her mother said, turning on her stool so that she sat facing her.

"What?"

"I have something to say to you. Now."

Eden looked up because of the tone of voice. This wasn't Edna talking. This was still the illustrious Dr. Trevoy, who meant to be heard.

"All right," Eden said, resting on her knees. "Say it."

"I'm not your mother."

Eden heard her perfectly, but the remark was so unheralded and so unexpected that, at first, her mind refused to take it in. And it was a simple enough statement.

I'm not your mother.

Eden went back to rolling up the sleeping bag, her mind racing, trying desperately to grasp what Edna had meant. She didn't say *I'm not a good mother*—which, if she had been struck suddenly by a flash of self-enlightenment, might have been expected. She said *I'm not* your *mother.*

I'm not your mother.

"Eden, did you hear me?"

"I heard you," Eden said quietly. She was still looking down at the sleeping bag. It surprised her to see that her hands were trembling. But what surprised her more was that, in spite of her initial shock, she believed this sudden pronouncement. Completely. Utterly. Without question. She believed it.

She forced herself to look into Edna Trevoy's eyes.

"And?" she asked, the calmness of her voice belying her shaking hands.

"And I thought you should know."

"Why?" Eden asked.

"Why?"

"Yes, *why?* Why are you telling me this? It's not like you to be this forthcoming. Your way is to sneak off in the middle of the night and let me wake up and find you long gone. Where did this sudden penchant for telling me the truth come from? Why now? *Why?*"

"Because it's time."

Eden threw up her hands. "It's *time?* Why is it time? Why didn't you tell me when I was a little kid—when I needed to understand the reason you were so indifferent? 'I'm not your mother' would have certainly explained it.

You are a real piece of work, you know that? My whole
life—*my whole life*—you've done things like this! I
thought once I was grown, I'd have a little peace. But, no!
You're still crashing around like a bull in a china shop,
aren't you? Breaking things right and left—but what the
hell! Edna Trevoy has to get where she's going, doesn't
she? And if some fragile little something happens to get
in the way—well, too damn bad!''

''Eden—''

''So what am I supposed to do with this pithy information, Mother? Oh, excuse me. It isn't 'Mother,' is it? I
don't know quite what I should call you—''

''Eden, don't.''

''What was it you said you wanted to do out here? Tie
up the loose ends? So. A major discovery *and* the truth
about your so-called daughter. I'm assuming everything's
all neatly knotted now—''

''I just want you to be happy!''

Eden laughed, because the truly incredible thing was
that Edna Trevoy probably believed her ridiculous assertion. How could she be happy knowing this? An indifferent
real mother was far better than no mother at all. Didn't
Edna realize that?

''Too late,'' Eden said. It would have been so easy for
her to have been happy if Edna Trevoy had been so inclined. A personal letter every now and then when she was
away at school. Something written by Edna herself—not
a memo from the archaeology department secretary telling
her that they didn't quite know where Dr. Trevoy was at
the moment and therefore they couldn't forward her
mail—hence the growing pile of letters there from her
daughter, all of them uncollected and unanswered in her
pigeonhole. In lieu of that, if a few written words were too
much of a chore, Eden would have been thrilled to have

even one photograph of the latest site. There were always plenty of photographs. But, no. No letters and no pictures. Her classmates hadn't even believed that she had a mother—much less one who was a professor of archaeo-astronomy. Little had she guessed how right they were.

"I know you're...upset," Edna said.

"Upset?" she said incredulously.

"In time you'll understand—"

Eden gave a short laugh. There wasn't enough time in the world for her to ever understand this. "So tell me. Why the big secret? If you're not my mother, then who is?"

"I don't know."

"You don't *know?* What am I then? A foundling?"

"Not exactly."

"What exactly?"

"You were...in peril."

"Of what?"

"Of not being born."

They stared at each other.

"And kindly Dr. Trevoy saved me, is that it?"

"Eden—"

"You know," Eden said, standing up. "I don't want to talk about this. I told Toomey earlier—the things that happened when you're a little kid—they don't really matter now—not at this late date. And they don't." She grabbed up as much of the equipment as she could carry and walked toward the crevice in the rocks.

"Eden, there's more," her used-to-be mother called after her.

"I don't want to hear any more," Eden said. "Not now. Not ever."

A truck was coming fast along the dirt track. Toomey could see the cloud of dust long before he actually heard it. There was nothing lost or haphazard about its approach. Whoever was driving it knew exactly where he was going and why.

He stood by the police utility vehicle and waited. He could see the truck better now. It was bleached and sand-blasted into a no-color gray like a hundred other trucks on the rez. The right front bumper had been knocked outward and upward into a kind of vehicular snarl. When it skidded to a stop, and the cloud of dust surrounding it finally settled, Toomey immediately recognized the old man driving. Billy George, who had known Toomey's father well and who had worked for years as a guide for Edna Trevoy.

"*Yah-ta-hey*, Billy," he called as the old man got out. He was immediately struck by the obvious frailness of yet another person from his childhood. In his mind Billy George, like Edna Trevoy, had remained vigorous and youthful, and it took him a moment to adjust to reality. "Still driving like a bat out of hell, I see," he said.

The old man laughed. "What you going to do, policeman? Give me a ticket way out here?"

"I might," Toomey said, smiling.

"Got to have a road before you can go handing out tickets," Billy said. "Don't see no road around here."

They stood for a moment appreciating each other's wit.

"You looking for Miss Edna?" Toomey asked, guessing that Billy George and his beat-up truck must have been the means by which Edna and her daughter had gotten out here.

Billy glanced at him, then off toward the crevice in the rocks. "You seen her?"

"She's still in the arroyo," Toomey said. "I've been advised to wait here."

Billy made a small sound of acknowledgment. "Best to

wait—the both of us. She find what she was looking for?'' he asked.

"She found what she thinks is a calendar."

"Might as well call it that then," Billy observed. "If Miss Edna thinks so."

Toomey agreed wholeheartedly. He certainly had no desire to oppose Edna Trevoy's archaeological conclusions. He'd had enough trouble opposing the *other* reason she'd come out here. And he still didn't know what that reason was. He had a letter in his shirt pocket, because Miss Edna had used every bit of emotional blackmail at her disposal to get him to put it there. He wasn't supposed to *do* anything with it, a fact that should have reassured him, but didn't. This letter business was nothing but trouble for Eden and for him, and Dr. Trevoy damn well knew it.

He chitchatted with Billy George—about family, the weather, the tribal council elections. And he watched the sun rise higher and higher. He couldn't wait around here much longer. Captain Becenti wanted to see him this morning. Period. Besides that, he was uneasy about whatever was taking place in the arroyo, and he didn't have enough information to even attempt to envision what that might be. The only thing he knew for certain was that Eden Trevoy was completely unsuspecting and that her mother was infinitely sad.

He wasn't doing a very good job at hiding his agitation, because Billy kept glancing at him.

"You in a hurry?" the old man finally asked.

"Yeah," Toomey said, fighting down the urge to pace.

"You going to arrest them for something?"

"No. I just have to make sure they get out of here okay."

"Then you ain't got to hang around," Billy said. "I'm here to do that. Miss Edna hired me to drive them back to her place. You can go look for somebody else to arrest. I hear the bootlegging is pretty bad around these parts."

"No kidding," Toomey said dryly, because this particular area was notorious for its traffic in illegal whiskey. "You're not in that bad business, are you, Billy?"

"Who me? No. Too damn old for that kind of trouble. Too damn old to even drink the stuff. Can't drink no more. Can't smoke. Doctor even says I can't eat Twinkies when I want to—and the women don't think I'm so cute now, either. Ain't much of a life."

"Maybe you should find yourself a woman who can't see so good. Maybe hide her glasses." Toomey made his suggestion with a straight face, but then they both laughed, and Billy patted him on the back.

"Miss Edna's coming out now," he said, looking sharply around.

The woman looked terrible. Both Billy and he stepped forward to help her.

"Wait," Toomey said to her, because she seemed so dazed and unfocused. He took her by the arm. "Wait, Miss Edna—"

"I just—want to—sit down," she said.

They put her into Billy's truck.

"Do you need a doctor?" Toomey asked. "I can radio the closest clinic and—"

"No," she said, patting his hand. "I know—what's wrong with me. And I know—what to do. It'll get better in a—minute. Will you go see about—Eden?" Her eyes met his briefly, then slid away.

But Eden was already coming out of the arroyo. She was loaded down with camping gear and cameras, none of which she would let him carry for her.

"I don't need any help," she kept saying.

Not with the equipment maybe, Toomey thought.

But she definitely needed help of some kind. She was so pale, as pale as her obviously ill mother.

"Are you——?"

"I don't need any help," she repeated, looking at him now, both determined and desperate.

He understood finally. She was hanging on by a thread, and having to deal with him was making it worse. He stood back out of the way.

"Benjamin," Edna called.

He moved to see what she wanted.

"Don't—forget," she said. "You—promised."

Chapter Three

Toomey missed his morning audience with Captain Becenti. When he finally arrived in Window Rock, the captain, according to Mary Skeets, was no longer in the building. Lieutenant Singer, on the other hand, was. And he was eagerly awaiting a certain young officer's arrival with every intention of passing on the grief Becenti had just given him.

Toomey had enough sense not to go in making excuses. He didn't say anything at all, not even when Lucas pointedly looked at his watch. He stood waiting while the lieutenant ostensibly shuffled papers.

"Well?" Lucas said after a time.

"Sir?" Toomey countered, not wanting to go anywhere near a question as broad as that one.

"What did you do with Dr. Trevoy?"

"Do?"

"Where is she, Toomey?" Lucas asked.

"She, ah, went back to her place, sir."

"I see. Did you offer to take her for medical treatment?"

"Yes, sir," Toomey said cautiously.

"And?"

"And she didn't want to see a doctor. She just wanted to go home."

"And you let Billy George take her," Lucas said. It wasn't a question.

Toomey sighed, but not as quietly as he'd intended.

"What?" Lucas said. "You think I only find out what you're up to when *you* tell me?"

"Yes, sir," Toomey said. "I mean, no, sir," he immediately amended.

"So what have you been doing in the meantime?"

"Meantime, sir?"

"Yes, meantime. Dr. Trevoy went with Billy George. Where did you go?"

"I took Dr. Trevoy's daughter to get her vehicle."

"Billy George was going to be driving right past it, wasn't he? I don't suppose it occurred to you to let him drop her off, or did you think your tribal police duties included running a personal shuttle service?"

"She wouldn't go with him, sir."

"Why not?"

"She and her mother had some kind of—something—an argument, I guess. Both women were really upset. Eden—the daughter—she wouldn't go with Dr. Trevoy. She asked me if I would take her to get her car. I couldn't very well leave her out there by herself."

Lucas stared at him. Toomey tried to look as at ease with his decision now as he had been when he made it. And he tried not to think of the ride back into town with Eden Trevoy. She had said absolutely nothing the entire trip. Not one word. And the whole time he'd had the distinct feeling that she was crying again—only this time it was without tears and without making a sound.

"Take the afternoon off," Lucas said abruptly, going back to his papers.

"Sir?" Toomey said, caught completely off guard.

"You were just coming off a ten-to-ten shift when you took it upon yourself to go looking for Dr. Trevoy. That was more than twenty-four hours ago. You look like hell, and you make enough mistakes when you're rested. Go home. Get some sleep."

"Yes, sir," he said, but he still didn't go. He had planned to suffer a lot more than this.

"Get going!"

"Yes, sir," Toomey said again.

He waited until he was out in the hall and the door was firmly closed behind him.

"Yes!" he whispered, in spite of the fact that he felt like hell, too. His head pounded with fatigue. Except for what little sleep he'd had in the arroyo, when *had* he slept last? He didn't quite remember.

His stomach growled, but food could wait. In his mind and in his heart he was already back at his almost completely restored, circa fifties, strategically placed, New Moon trailer. The shadows from the red rock monoliths and the one cottonwood tree would be just about right now so that the bedroom half of the trailer would be deep in shade. Cool. Perfect for sleeping, if he turned on his one oscillating fan. He was scheduled to be off duty for the next two days. When he got home, he could stretch out in his underwear—careful not to bang his head on the downward slope of the real-wood-paneled wall—and sleep for hours. And he would *not* worry about Eden Trevoy.

"Hold it!" Mary Skeets called as he was about to go out the door.

"I'm not here, Mary," he called back. "I'm home asleep."

"Well, your desk is here," she said. "It's on the back of the truck and it's supposed to rain. It's not in great shape as it is, but if you want to let it get wet, too, that's up to you."

He pushed the door open and looked outside. Mary Skeets, irrepressible dispatcher and weather forecaster, was right as usual. The thunderheads were already forming in the northwest.

He didn't want to let the desk get wet. He had lobbied for something to call his own for far too long to leave it exposed to elements—no matter what kind of shape it was in—and it was in pretty bad shape, even for someone as desperate for a piece of office furniture as he was.

"Where did you find this thing?" he asked Mary, who had tagged along to supervise the unloading.

"Officially, it's a law enforcement building desk. We loaned it to one of the chapter houses for some reason. Now we're getting it back. Just for you."

"I'm honored," he said, helping Joey Nez, the other officer Mary had conscripted, to get the desk down off the truck and carry it into the building.

"Well, you should be. I think this is the one Lucas Singer used when he first joined the tribal police—so it's practically a holy relic. Look—" she said, waving her hands over it as if she were showcasing a fine piece of furniture on a TV quiz show. "It's got handles on the drawers and everything."

"Amazing," Joey said, huffing and puffing to hold up his end until Mary got around to the side door she was supposed to open.

"I see your hair is growing out," Mary said as Toomey shuffled past.

"Don't start with me, Mary," he warned her. "Do *not* start with me." He had heard enough remarks about hair to last him a lifetime. He didn't even want to think about his most recent haircut—or Lucas Singer's reaction to it.

"Hey, I think it's great the way you let your little sister practice on your head. You could have gotten a buzz cut and gotten rid of it, but you didn't. You're a good brother, Benjamin. Hairstyling is where the money's at these days—and she's bound to get better at it. But I think I'd volunteer Joey here for her next one."

"She'll have to catch me first," Joey said over his shoulder. "Your sister is a good-looking girl, Ben—but she ain't no barber."

"Well, it looks okay now," Mary said, holding open another door. "Kind of...oh, I don't know. What's that magazine—*GQ?*"

"Or *Sheep Clipper's Gazette*," Joey offered.

"Oh, yeah, very funny—" Toomey said.

He abruptly set his end of the desk down, precipitating a strong protest from Joey.

"I'll be right back," Toomey said over his shoulder, because he could see Eden Trevoy standing just inside the front doors—when she should be well on her way to Albuquerque.

He walked directly up to her, surprising her because he came out of a side hallway when she was looking in the other direction. "What's wrong?" he asked without prelude, a question he should have asked before they ever left the arroyo. He had thought she looked stressed then. It was nothing compared to the way she looked now. Even so, she was still pretty, too pretty and too affluent looking not to immediately turn heads in a police station.

"I think you know," she said. Her voice wavered, but she didn't look like she was going to cry. She looked angry.

"No, I don't," he said. "What's the—?"

"I was just going to fade away into the sunset—slink quietly back to Albuquerque where I belong," she interrupted. "But then I decided I'm not going to let this go. I have something to say to you and I'm going to say it."

In spite of her agitation, the soft voice he'd noted in the arroyo was still very much in evidence. And Mary Skeets and Joey, and any number of police personnel were working hard to hear it—not to mention several arrestees and a few members of the public.

"I think I can find a room where we can talk—" he said, attempting to steer her away from the crowd.

"No, thank you. This is going to be short and sweet. I just want you to know how much I resent your insinuating yourself into my personal business. You have no right to do that. None."

He attempted a laugh, because he was caught completely off guard. "I don't know what you mean."

"I mean that the next time you and Edna decide to have one of your little tête-à-têtes, I want you to leave *me* out of it. I don't want to be the topic of your conversations and I don't want you or anyone else knowing anything about my personal life."

"I don't know anything about your personal life. What are—?"

"Don't play dumb with me!" she cried, turning whatever few disinterested heads remained in their direction. He could see Lucas Singer come out of his office.

"Edna told you! It's very obvious that the two of you are bosom buddies—"

"I don't know what you're talking about," Toomey said, trying not to lose his temper.

"She paid you, didn't she?"

"Paid—?"

"I saw her give you the envelope. What was *that* for? Keeping her little secrets?"

"Your mother didn't pay me."

"I saw her!"

"No, you didn't," Toomey said evenly. "What you saw—"

"You knew about the adoption," she said.

"What adoption!"

"Mine!" she cried. *"Mine!"*

"Eden," he said, trying to take her arm. "This whole conversation is crazy. I *don't* know what you're talking about."

She stared at him, her mouth trembling. "You're a liar."

"I'm going to forget you said that because you're obviously upset. There may be a liar somewhere in whatever is going on between you and your mother—but it is *not* me. Understand? The envelope you saw is *yours*. I'm supposed to keep it for you until you ask for it. Do you want it? It's in my vehicle. I'll go get it for you—"

She didn't answer him. She abruptly turned and slammed out of the building, leaving him standing.

"Guess not," he said to himself.

"Toomey!" Lucas yelled down the hall, and Toomey gave a sharp sigh. All in all, afternoon off or not, he had had better days.

"Don't you people have work to do?" Lucas asked pointedly, dispersing the audience—which was fine with Toomey. Generally speaking, he preferred the you-know-what to hit the fan without one. People were going to be talking about Benjamin Toomey's adventure with the

missing Dr. Trevoy and the way her rich daughter came
right into the law enforcement building and gave him hell
for weeks. His mother would have questions. His grandmother. His aunts. His boss already had them.

"I thought I sent you home," Lucas said as Toomey
walked closer.

"Yes, sir," he said. "I'm going."

"What was that all about?"

"It's personal, sir," Toomey said.

"Well, you keep your 'personal' doings out of this office, you understand?"

"Yes, sir."

"It's hard enough to keep people on track without you
giving these impromptu floor shows."

"Yes, sir," he said again.

"Well?"

"Sir?"

"Go home!"

Toomey meant to do that very thing—but Joey Nez,
who was never one not to finish what he started, still
waited by the holy desk. They moved it with considerable
difficulty into a small space by one of the file cabinets, a
location that would likely require Toomey to stand up
every time somebody wanted something in the drawer
marked "PQR." And word of his newly acquired desk
was spreading rapidly. His co-workers were already bringing stacks of rubber-banded files—*his* cases—the ones he
had scattered around on various and sundry borrowed
desktops.

He sat down on the chair Mary scrounged for him and
took off the rubber bands, diligently alphabetizing the records in spite of his weariness and putting them into a neat
pile. Then he opened the drawers to see if anything useful
had made the transfer from the chapter house, because he

was innately curious and because he was working hard
now to keep from thinking about the events of the last
twenty-four hours and Eden Trevoy. Yesterday at this time
she didn't exist for him, except as a vague memory from
his childhood, a memory of a little dark-haired girl who
smiled shyly when he ran fast or jumped high. Today she
was—

He didn't know quite what she was. He only knew that
she had replaced her mother as the reason for the overwhelming disharmony he was feeling. Eden Trevoy
thought he was a liar and had said so. She thought he had
deceived her somehow. It pained him deeply to be accused
of such a thing, even by a stranger. Had he deceived her?
He didn't really know. He certainly hadn't been told anything about an adoption. He had the letter, and if that con-
stituted a deception of some kind, then he supposed he
must be guilty, albeit unwittingly.

No, he wasn't guilty, he abruptly decided. He only *felt*
guilty—hence all the rampant disharmony. He needed to
get away by himself for a time. He needed to purify himself with a sweat bath. He needed to center himself with
the ancient chants his grandfather had taught him. He
needed to really think about this situation.

Or he needed not to think about it at all.

The top right-hand drawer was stuck. He got it open far
enough to get his hand in. He could feel a ruler—a plastic
one—jammed way in the back. He kept pulling and pushing and reaching, trying to dislodge it. His fingers touched
something else, and he pulled it out. A disintegrating book
of matches, nearly to the point of "holy relic" status like
the desk.

He kept fiddling. His fingers touched more paper and he
pulled hard. A Navajo Tribal Police work schedule for one
Officer Lucas Singer. So. It had been the lieutenant's desk.

He reached back in, pulling hard on the ruler until it snapped in two and the drawer slid all the way out. Nothing much left inside it, he noted. Some paper clips. Pieces of the offending red plastic ruler. Chewing gum wrappers—no used gum, happily. The inside of the drawer had a puddle of something dried but still sticky and some kind of rectangular piece of paper stuck firmly in the middle of it. He pulled on it until it came loose and turned it over. It was a color snapshot of two people, with most of one of the two subjects peeled off by the spill. He looked at it carefully. Nobody he knew. A blond-haired girl smiling into the camera and the remains of someone who was probably male and Navajo. The picture didn't look all that recent. Maybe the girl was a VISTA Volunteer, he thought idly. She had that official so-happy-to-be-here-to-save-you look. The rez used to be crawling with them. There was something written on the back, but the ink had smeared. A name? Sandra?

"Lucas is about to sally forth," Mary told him in passing. "I wouldn't still be here if he'd already told me to go home twice."

"Roger that," he said. "Thanks."

He put the photograph back into the drawer, closed it firmly and prudently left by a side exit.

The New Moon trailer was half in the shade as he had expected, but he didn't go immediately inside. He parked the police utility vehicle in its usual spot and sat in it for a moment before he got out.

What is it with Eden Trevoy?

The thought popped into his head in spite of his resolve not to concern himself any longer with things that were none of his business.

"Not your problem, man," he said, getting out of the vehicle. He knew that without a doubt. The real difficulty came from realizing how much he *wanted* it to be his problem. He wanted Eden Trevoy to tell him exactly what was wrong. He wanted to listen to her and then give her his sage advice, which would somehow make things infinitely better and which would earn him her undying gratitude.

And he was an idiot.

He let himself into the trailer, feeling a certain degree of pleasure as he always did when he opened the door. He put down his keys and the clipboard that had Eden's letter firmly secured on it, and he began looking through an upper kitchen cabinet for something to eat, something of the junk food persuasion, the kind that old Billy George couldn't eat anymore. He found a package of chocolate cupcakes, and he poured some milk into the huge glass he'd won tossing pennies at the Navajo Tribal Fair in Ship Rock. But he didn't stay in the trailer to eat. He was still too agitated, and he took his improvised meal outside and sat down on the steps in the shade, savoring the quiet and a strong breeze that rustled the nearby cottonwood.

He still couldn't believe his luck at finding this trailer to live in. He had bought it from an elderly couple passing through Window Rock on their way down from Canyon de Chelly and over to the Chaco Canyon ruins. The wife had a weak heart, and she had gotten worse on the trip and had to be flown back to her doctors in Baltimore. The old man had wanted to sell the trailer in a hurry, believing—knowing—that the two of them wouldn't be traveling in it again. The price had been right—even the bank thought so—and Ben Toomey had become an official home owner. He had picked out a spot where he wanted to put a trailer long before he ever owned one, raising both his mother and his grandmother's eyebrows, because he had wanted to live out here alone instead of living in the Toomey-Benally compound with the rest of the clan.

The truth was simply that he needed to be away from everybody else, particularly since he'd become a tribal policeman. He had always enjoyed his solitude, even as a child. He loved his family. He wanted to be close to them—but not too close. Being a policeman was emotionally hard at times. He had seen things—bad things—that stayed on his mind for days afterward. But it was part of the job, and it was something he had to work through by himself. And he didn't want six pairs of worried eyes watching him while he struggled to come to terms with the ugliness in the world.

He spent almost all of his free time trying to restore the trailer to its former glory, one paycheck at a time, sanding and refinishing the stem-to-stern real-wood paneling to a warm patina, going to the library and poring over the bound copies of old fifties magazines, looking at the New Moon trailer ads therein so he could see how the thing was supposed to look. He and the woman at the library information desk had spent a lot of quality time together on that one. She hadn't batted an eyelash when he told her what he wanted to know—that was one of the reasons he liked libraries. One could *not* shock a librarian with a sincere request for information, no matter what the topic. Where else could he go and make somebody happy just by being ignorant?

He wondered from time to time what had happened to the old couple, if the man regretted having let the trailer go and if he would be pleased by what Toomey had done to it. Toomey had gotten everything to the point were he felt free to "entertain" his big family and his tribal police friends from time to time. Actually, his parties were kind of "work-for-food" affairs. Everyone he invited helped

him with his current restoration project, for which he fed
them to within an inch of their lives. His maternal grandmother, Sadie Benally, who would cook at the drop of a
hat, loved these gatherings. He smiled to himself, thinking
about the way she would come early and order him around
until a huge and wonderful meal had been put together.
She was the reason an invitation to Ben Toomey's was so
highly prized—even if it did involve sanding and scraping.

He sighed and looked up at the sky. It was indeed going
to rain. He could smell it coming. He finished the last
cupcake and drank the milk.

Not bad, he thought, but he didn't mean the meager
meal. He meant the fact that he'd been able to go ten—
maybe even fifteen—minutes without thinking about Eden
Trevoy. What little he knew about her situation, he did *not*
understand—no matter how hard he tried. He had never
heard even a whisper about an adoption; he had absolutely
no idea what *that* was about. If he'd known earlier, he
would have asked Billy George if he had heard about Eden
Trevoy's having been adopted. He still might.

He gave a heavy sigh. There was nothing logical or
orderly in any of this business. And he was too tired to
deal with it any longer. He went inside and straight to bed,
falling into a deep sleep that was only occasionally dis-
turbed by thunder and rain and dreams of a dark-haired
young woman who wouldn't listen.

Chapter Four

"Lucas is waiting for you," Mary Skeets told him on Wednesday when he came in to work.

Now what? he thought. He was here on the right day. And he wasn't late—or early. He was working 10:00 a.m. to 10:00 p.m. now instead of the other way around, and he was right on time. He hated to start a shift with a dressing-down. He just hated it.

"He wants to see you first thing," Mary persisted.

First thing. Wonderful.

"You know what's going on?" he asked her.

"Yes," she said.

"But you're not about to tell me, right?"

"Right," she said, answering the telephone.

He went down the hall to Lucas's office and knocked on the closed door. Surely Eden Trevoy hadn't filed some kind of complaint. Insinuating oneself into somebody else's personal life might be uncouth—but it wasn't against any tribal police regulations. He hoped.

"In!" Lucas said from the other side.

Toomey pushed the door open.

"Toomey—good," Lucas said, barely looking up from his paperwork. "I wanted to make sure you knew about Dr. Trevoy."

"Dr. Trevoy?"

"She died," he said bluntly.

Died?

"I...no. I didn't know."

Died?

"That's all," Lucas said. "I just wanted you to be advised. You can go."

"Yes, sir."

Toomey turned and walked to the door. Had she gotten all her loose ends tied? he wondered crazily, trying to absorb the news. If not, she'd verified her calendar at least, and he supposed that was something.

"Sir," he asked abruptly. "Do you know what happened? Do you know if her daughter was with her?"

Lucas looked up from the papers. "I don't know anything about her daughter. I just know the woman died. Apparently it was not that unexpected. The university is having a memorial service at the Gallup branch."

"When?"

"I don't know. I didn't ask."

"I'd like to go, sir. I'd like the time off if I'm working."

"I thought you followed the Old Ways. What are you going to do at something like that?" Lucas asked. It was a topic they'd covered before. Lucas Singer had his misgivings about how steeped in Navajo traditionalism a police officer could be and still do his job. Thus far, Toomey had managed. He had put all his childhood teachings aside when it was necessary. He had even dealt with the dead when he had to. He still wouldn't whistle after sundown, and he might even be tempted to turn around if a coyote crossed his path when he left on a trip—but Lucas didn't have to know that.

"There are no dead bodies at a memorial service, sir," he said.

"I suppose your wanting to go to this thing has got something to do with her so-called disappearance."

"Not...exactly, sir," Toomey said. He still expected Lucas to ask him specifically what had happened in the arroyo, but he didn't. And it wouldn't have done him any good. The bottom line was that Toomey didn't *know* what had happened.

The lieutenant continued to look at him. Toomey could almost feel him deciding.

"Find out when it is, then," Lucas said finally. "And we'll see."

It took Mary Skeets about five minutes to get all the details from somebody in Gallup and pass them on to Lucas—except, of course, the one thing Toomey wanted to know. Would Eden Trevoy be there?

But there were no pronouncements regarding his request immediately forthcoming. He knew better than to ask. Lucas would give his permission—or not. And Ben Toomey's job was to patiently wait.

Mary Skeets gave him the verdict at the beginning of his shift the next day, and on Friday afternoon, Toomey left the law enforcement building to drive to the memorial service in Gallup—with Lucas Singer's blessing, actually. Not only had Toomey been given the time off to attend, but he had also been instructed to wear his best uniform and to act as an official representative for the Navajo Tribal Police. He filed the entire experience away for future reference—just in case a miracle occurred and he made it to a supervisory position and an office of his own.

Never *ever* miss an opportunity to do PR.

The service was supposed to take place in a small amphitheater-slash-classroom on the UNM campus, but he had some difficulty finding it. College campuses never seemed to take into account that there might be people roaming about the place who didn't know where they were going. He was finally directed to the right building and the right door by a giggling girl student who was clearly impressed by a man in uniform. He had never been one not to appreciate overt female approval, and he was still smiling when he opened the amphitheater door. He had to abruptly remind himself what he was here for.

What exactly *am* I here for? he wondered as he climbed the aisle steps looking for a place to sit. He had liked the late professor certainly. She had always been kind to him—except maybe in this last gesture of hers, in making him the keeper of that letter. But he hadn't come today simply out of respect for her. Mostly, he wanted the chance to talk to her daughter. He wanted the chance to defend himself, even if this wasn't the time or place to do it.

He uprooted a number of people to get to the only empty seat near the front. It occurred to him as he sat down that there was a very good chance that Eden might not even be here. Given how little time she would have had to patch up the quarrel—or whatever it was—with her mother, it was more likely that this would be a gathering of students and the professor's associates only. He immediately began to scan the amphitheater. There was a podium down front. And two large baskets of flowers. And a piano. But no Eden Trevoy in any of the first-row seats.

More and more people were filing in, students and faculty as he had expected, and a few persons he recognized from the tourist bureau and the city government. Someone—a redheaded girl with ugly shoes and really long hair—sat down at the piano and began to play. The music was vaguely familiar—a popular old love song, he decided, and something he wouldn't have expected to hear on this somber occasion.

"Oh, it's 'Tenderly,'" someone said behind him. "You remember that old blue music box—that round, metal thing Miss Edna always took with her on the digs. It played that song. Every evening after supper. 'Tenderly' over and over and over."

"Professor Shipp offered me twenty bucks one time—" a different voice interjected "—to steal the damn thing and drop it off a cliff."

The group laughed appreciatively, then grew quiet again.

The music box must have been after his time, Toomey thought. He had no memory of such a thing, and he would have remembered the "Tenderly" episode of the professor's life. Funny. He would have never thought of her as having a favorite song—favorite beer maybe, favorite cigarette certainly, but not a song.

The auditorium was crowded now, standing room only, but nothing was happening. The piano player finished her rendition of Miss Edna's favorite tune—her own personal remembrance and tribute, Toomey realized—and rejoined the audience.

People were beginning to stir restlessly—Toomey among them. Small pockets of conversation sprang up around him. Finally, several professor types entered, one of them walking directly to the podium.

"Ladies and gentlemen," he began, making the sound system squeal until somebody rushed up to tune out the feedback. "Thank you for coming today on this very sad occasion…"

Toomey stopped listening. He kept looking at the lower doors. A few more stragglers drifted in—none of them Eden.

The man at the podium finished his remarks, and various people in the audience, one after another, began a solitary walk down to the microphone to speak. Most of their anecdotes were humorous, filled with "Miss Edna-isms" that made Toomey smile. The woman was one of a kind, there was no denying that.

Another man came to the podium. He, too, had the threadbare and out-of-style look of those too engrossed in something academic to pay attention to current fashion trends. Or perhaps professors were like tribal cops and just didn't make enough money to dress for success.

The man began simply enough, but it was soon clear—to Toomey at least—that he had come to bury Edna Trevoy, not to praise her.

This must be Shipp or Hill, he thought, one of the professors who had put Toomey's "virgin ears" in danger.

The man droned on, enumerating the esteemed Dr. Trevoy's decidedly unorthodox ways. Then he lamented her endless and subsequently fruitless quest for professional validation, her failing health, and finally her ambitious but ultimately failed dreams.

"Very sad," he assured the gathering. "Very sad indeed—to work so diligently, so faithfully and never—"

Toomey had had about all he could stand. He gave a quiet sigh and stood, waiting respectfully until the man noticed.

"Excuse me, sir," he said when the man looked in his direction. "I just wanted to say that the doctor did find what she was looking for."

The man smiled slightly, but he didn't mean it.

"And you are?" he asked.

"Officer Ben Toomey—Navajo Tribal Police. She did find it, and I was just thinking," he plunged on, ignoring the heads still turning in his direction. "This would be a good time for that announcement to be made. Everyone gathered here to honor her should know that her faith in her own hypothesis, her...dream, if you will, was justified."

"And you have the...authority to make that announcement?" the man at the podium asked.

"I was there," Toomey said—which wasn't exactly an answer.

"And what was it Dr. Trevoy found?" a woman two rows down turned and asked—a question Toomey sensed would not have come from the man at the podium.

"Proof that the Old Ones had some concept of astronomy. A calendar—one used by the Anasazi to indicate the summer solstice."

"A calendar," the man repeated, drawing attention back to the podium. The tone was condescending at best.

"Well, she didn't actually find it on this trip," Toomey qualified.

"No, I shouldn't think so."

"Actually, she's known about it for years. This final trip was just to verify its purpose and to document the manifestation of the Anasazi 'sun serpent' on June twenty-first—the summer solstice. She believed that the 'sun serpent' would be the indicator in this case, rather than the so-called 'sun dagger'—which is the basis for other, similar discoveries," he added in case the man still thought he was winging it. "As you probably know, she also thought there was an important reason why the sun serpent was on so much of the pottery. A videotape was made of the event—and numerous still photographs—"

"Yes, I see," the man said, cutting him off. "Well—thank you very much for sharing that with us."

"Oh, you're welcome," Toomey said as he sat down. My pleasure.

The testimonies continued, more anecdotes about the eccentric but beloved professor, and the revelation that years ago Dr. Trevoy had used a major portion of her considerable trust fund to set up an anonymous scholarship for Native American students. Toomey suddenly remembered a time in his junior year when his financial situation had become so dire and part-time jobs so scarce that he was going to have to leave school. And he made the connection between the financial aid his student advisor had somehow "found" for him and a remark Edna Trevoy had made that day at the arroyo.

I kept up with you when you were at the university...you didn't know that, did you?

No, Miss Edna, he thought. *I didn't.*

He hadn't bothered to find out where his sudden windfall had come from. He had merely given profound thanks to whatever deity happened to be responsible and signed the papers. But sitting here now, listening to the eulogies, he had no doubt that it was Edna Trevoy who deserved his gratitude.

The memorial service finally ended, and he filed out with everyone else, wondering as he went what Miss Edna would have made of all this. He walked down the hallway and outside into the bright sunlight. He was relieved that the service was over. He had made his gesture of respect, and he felt better for it, but he still hadn't regained his harmony. In the chorus of his life, somebody or something was singing decidedly off-key—he himself perhaps. And he didn't know quite what to do about it, except to go back to Window Rock where he belonged.

"Officer Toomey," a woman's voice called across the parking lot, and he turned around. Eden Trevoy was walking in his direction. He waited for her to catch up with him, surprised that he had missed seeing her in the auditorium and that she would actually want to speak to him. He earnestly hoped that this overt gesture of hers wasn't the start of Round Two.

"I'm very sorry for your loss," he said when she reached him. She was pale and clearly exhausted, the paleness enhanced by the black dress she was wearing. She let her eyes meet his, but only briefly.

"Thank you," she said. "And thank you for what you did in there."

"I didn't do anything."

"Except cut Professor Shipp off at the knees," she said. She gave a slight smile. "Edna would have been ecstatic. He was *not* one of her favorite people."

But her smile immediately faded. They stood there in silence. He didn't want to mention the last time they had met, and apparently neither did she. The wind whipped her dark hair about her face, and he had to suppress the urge to reach up and brush a strand out of her eyes.

"I didn't think you were here," he offered finally.

"I came in late—by the rear door. I was sitting way in the back. Well—I just wanted to thank you. I have to go," she said abruptly, turning away.

"Wait," he said. "If there's anything I can do—"

"No," she said quickly. "There's nothing." She looked up at him, holding his gaze too long for his comfort or hers.

"I really have to go," she said. "The department head

says Edna's place needs to be cleared out right away—I understand university housing is really tight.''

"Who's the department head? Shipp?''

"Yes,'' she said, smiling briefly again.

"You're going there now?'' Toomey asked.

"I don't think I have much choice.''

"Do you want some help?''

The question surprised her—and him. His time constraints were such that he had no business making the offer; Lucas Singer would have a fit.

Another fit.

What the hell, he thought. It was too late to withdraw the offer now.

He was standing close enough to her so that he could just smell her scent, the soft female essence that was her. She gave a heavy sigh.

"Was that a yes or a no?'' he asked.

Another brief smile got away from her, but like the others, it quickly faded. "It was a no,'' she said. "Thank you, but I don't need any help.''

He stood and watched her walk away, waiting to see if she looked back at him. She didn't, but he made up his mind, anyway. And he already knew what he would tell the lieutenant. He would tell him the truth.

Toomey's offer of help had been gently made—not too surprising considering that at their last meeting Eden had called him a liar. But there was nothing tentative about it, and she didn't doubt his sincerity. The truth of the matter was that she did want help—perhaps even his help—but she just couldn't bring herself to say so. She didn't want to pack up Edna's things alone, and she didn't want to have to do it with some stranger from the university, or worse, someone she knew, like Shipp. If she had let

Toomey come with her, she wouldn't have had to keep up appearances. She wouldn't have had to talk to him at all if she didn't feel like it—Toomey wasn't someone who was threatened by a lack of conversation. She hadn't known him for very long, but she did know that.

But it was too late now. She arrived at Edna's apartment with but one goal in mind. To work as quickly as possible and to get out. She never wanted to see this part of New Mexico again.

The apartment was located in a long, one-story cement-block building, surrounded by a treeless and once-paved parking lot that was now mostly sand. There were no cars around. She parked near the front door and got out, squinting in the bright sunlight. As long as she had lived in this part of the country, she still couldn't remember that she needed sunglasses.

She unlocked the door and pushed it open, and she stood there for a moment, bracing herself before she went in. The inside of the apartment was unbearably hot and stuffy and smelled of Edna's stale cigarette smoke. None of the one- and two-bedroom apartments had air conditioners, except at the occupant's expense. And, of course, the no-frills Edna hadn't opted for that one small amenity.

Eden left the front door open. There was a ceiling fan, and she pulled the dangling string to turn it on. She kept thinking about Toomey. She was constantly changing her mind about him. At first she had thought him nice look-ing—certainly handsome enough for her to have taken a number of pictures of him in the arroyo. But then later, when she invaded his workplace for the express purpose of calling him names, she had thought not. In any event, she was no longer upset with him. She had gotten past that, even before he took it upon himself to liven up the memorial service by quietly putting Shipp in his place. She understood now—and perhaps she had at the time—that she had taken all the hurt and anger she had felt at yet another one of Edna's betrayals, and she had unfairly directed it toward Ben Toomey.

But she wasn't inclined to apologize, regardless of the fact that she had behaved badly. She never apologized. Until now she had never had a reason to. She had never let her emotions get the best of her like this before.

She stood looking around her. There wasn't a great deal to be done. Edna Trevoy had been embarrassed by her family's wealth. She herself had required very little, and except for her clothes and a few personal items, she had been perfectly content to live out of cardboard boxes. There were a number of them stacked and stored around the walls. Eden began to carefully collect what few belongings she could find in the drawers and cabinets, packing them into the boxes wherever she could find the space. She worked steadily and unsentimentally. She was completely focused on the job at hand, because she couldn't allow herself to dredge up any memories. She would cry if she did, and there was no earthly purpose in that.

She half expected that Shipp would come by to supervise—in case she tried to abscond with something that belonged to the university. After a while she realized that she didn't see the video camera or the tapes—especially the tapes—in any of the boxes where they should have been. Nor did she see Edna's red notebook—''Mr. Memory,'' she always called it. Eden wondered if Shipp had already been here. At the memorial service, he had seemed more than a little annoyed by Toomey's revelation—but surely the man wouldn't have come in here and taken away the only concrete evidence of Edna's find.

She sighed heavily. Of course he would. Professional jealousy sometimes ran rampant among the professors—

even the adopted-and-then-banished-to-boarding-school daughter of an academic knew that.

She began dumping some of the boxes out. There was no red notebook and no videotapes.

"What's wrong?" someone said as she was about to dump another box. She looked around sharply. Toomey stood in the open doorway.

"What are you doing here?" she asked, both annoyed by his intrusion and relieved to see him.

"I've been here for a while," he said.

"That's not an answer."

"Okay. I've been sitting in the parking lot trying to decide how I could convince you that I'm not a stalker."

"That's not an answer, either."

"No? Well—how about this. I've been drafted into this...situation between you and your mother—against my will *and* against my better judgment—and I don't know how to get out of it."

She continued to look at him. *Better,* she thought. But still not the whole truth.

"I brought the letter," he said finally. "In case you wanted it."

"I don't know if I want it or not," she said truthfully, recognizing that this was the bottom line.

He looked around at the upturned boxes. "You lose something?"

"I can't find the tapes of the 'sun serpent.' I can't find any tapes at all. I guess she must have returned the video camera to the department, but the tapes—all of her tapes—should be in one of these boxes."

"Maybe she put them someplace else."

"I can't find her red notebook, either," she said.

"Maybe someone from the university took both of them for safekeeping."

"That's what I'm afraid of."

She began to put everything back into the boxes. "I don't know why I should even care—but I—" She broke off and sighed again.

"Is there somebody you can ask?"

"Nobody but Shipp," she said.

"Well—if I know the one who died, the tapes and the notebook are exactly where she wants them to be. And even if Shipp did take them, he can't really prove he found the sun serpent because he's not going to know where the arroyo is. Nobody knows that but me—and maybe Billy George. And we aren't talking. I tell you what I would do, though. I'd go over Shipp's head. I'd write formal letters advising all the university powers that be that the video-tapes are missing and I'd state exactly what's on them. Maybe suggest that you plan to run an ad in the newspapers offering a reward for their return. Make sure a lot of people know they're gone—anything that will make it hard for Shipp to suddenly produce a video and claim the discovery as his. That way, if he's got them, he can't use them. If he doesn't, maybe somebody will let you know where they are."

She thought the advice was excellent—but she couldn't quite bring herself to say so. He took the box she had just filled out of her hands.

"I'll put this in your car—if you won't think I'm trying to insinuate myself into your personal life."

She looked at him for a moment, trying to decide if she wanted to pick up the gauntlet he had just thrown down.

No, she decided. She didn't.

"Thank you," she said, clearly taking him by surprise.

He carried the box out to the car. She stood watching him, and she waited until he had made several more trips.

"You were the only Navajo person at the memorial service," she said abruptly. "I was surprised. I thought my...I thought Edna had a lot of Navajo friends."

"They may not have known about the service," he said. "I wouldn't have if my lieutenant hadn't told me about it. And there's the taboo."

"What taboo?"

"The Navajo taboo regarding the dead. A traditional Navajo—someone who lives by the Old Ways—fears the dead and the place where the person died. All the dead person's belongings are taboo. Even the name of the dead person isn't spoken aloud—in case the ghost—the *chindi*—hears it and comes to do harm."

"But I thought you were traditional—Edna said you were. You came to the memorial service."

"It wasn't...comfortable for me, but I made the choice a long time ago to try to live in both worlds. Most of the time I can do it—no problem. And I know the difference between a memorial service and a funeral. A lot of the People who worked with her might not have. And even if they did, there would still be the thing of being in a place where the dead person's name would be spoken."

"You came here," she persisted, because she suddenly wanted to understand everything about his motives. And some part of her kept wondering why she was having to work so hard to be civil to him—when all she really wanted to do was put her head on his shoulder and cry. He was the only person in this world who had any idea how difficult her relationship with Edna had been, and he was the only one who might understand how much she would miss her. She had lost her mother twice in the span of a few days, and her heart was breaking.

"Well, I knew she died in the hospital," he said.

"But her things are here. You're carrying her boxes and you said the belongings were taboo."

He looked at her a long moment. "I want to help you if I can," he said simply.

It wasn't the answer she expected. It wasn't the answer she deserved. It was simply the truth; she knew that instinctively, too.

But his kindness made her feel so...defensive somehow.

"Why?" she asked. "Why should *you* want to help *me?*"

"Because of *her,* I guess. She was good to my family and to me. And I think she probably paid for part of my schooling with that anonymous scholarship she set up."

She stood looking at him and then gave a quiet sigh. "She didn't even have a funeral. Did you know that?"

"No."

"I don't even know where she's buried. She made her own arrangements with somebody or other. There was no—anything as far as I know. She's just...gone."

"Maybe she borrowed that from us," he said.

"From you?"

"From the Old Ways. That's kind of how it's done. Billy George might have taken care of all that for her."

She stared at him, holding his gaze until he looked away. "What's next?" he asked.

She handed him another cardboard box.

"The infamous music box," Toomey said, looking inside it.

"What?"

"The music box," he said, tilting the box so she could see it. He made no attempt to remove it.

"This must be the one that plays 'Tenderly,'" he said. "I heard some of the students talking about it at the memorial service, about how she drove everybody crazy with it. She always took it with her on the digs and she would play it over and over after supper."

Eden reached to lift it out, recognizing it immediately. "I gave this to her for Mother's Day—the first Mother's Day after she'd sent me away to boarding school. I didn't think she—" She abruptly stopped and turned away, clutching the music box tightly.

"She keeps doing that," she said after a moment. She took a deep breath and turned around again.

"Doing what?"

"Changing. Every time I think I finally know who she is—was—there's another revelation of some kind and I find out I don't know anything about her at all." She abruptly put the music box back into the cardboard box. "She said she didn't—" She stopped, realizing she was about to reveal just the kind of personal information she'd been so adamant that she didn't want him to know.

He didn't prod her to continue, but she found suddenly that she wanted to tell him this.

She looked up at him. "She said she didn't know who my real mother was."

"Maybe it's in the letter."

"Have you read it?" she asked, knowing the question would likely offend him.

"No, I haven't read it. I haven't read it, and I don't know why your mother wanted me to keep it."

"She wasn't my mother."

"In the way that counted, she was."

"What? Patting me on the head every now and then? Giving me money? Sending me to school? If that's the criteria, she's as much your mother as mine."

"Eden—" It was obvious that he was exasperated with her, just as it was obvious that she had been mistaken. He didn't understand. At all.

But he kept whatever remark he was about to make to himself. "You want to put anything else in this box?" he asked, his eyes looking somewhere over the top of her head.

She picked up a few remaining books and stuffed them inside. He took the box out to the car, and when he returned, he had a folded white envelope in his hand. He held it out to her, and after a moment she took it. Her name was scribbled on the front in Edna's spidery handwriting.

"I'm going now," he said. "I think I've left enough room for you to see around the boxes, but drive carefully—and have a nice life."

He didn't wait for her response.

"Officer Toomey," she called when he was well out the door.

He turned and stood waiting. She had to force herself to say it.

"I'm...sorry."

"For what?"

"For...taking everything out on you. None of this is your fault. I know that. But I..." She took a deep breath. It was easier the second time. "I'm sorry," she said again.

"Yeah, well, I don't think either one of us is ever going to figure her out. I meant what I said—about helping if I could. You know where I'll be."

She gave a slight smile at his second but more oblique reference to her visit to the law enforcement building in Window Rock.

"Would you—could you stay until I read this?"

"Yeah, okay," he said.

She looked down at the letter, grateful that he hadn't asked why she wanted him there. She would have been very hard-pressed to tell him—when she didn't know herself.

She tore open the envelope. There was only one page.

"My dear Eden," it began. "This is all I know about your real parents…"

She kept reading, straight to the end, then read it again.

"This can't be true," she said, more to herself than to Toomey. She abruptly turned away from him and began to pace the room. "She's wrong. She has to be wrong."

"Are you okay?" he asked.

"Oh, I'm just *fine*," she said sarcastically. She abruptly crumpled the letter in her fist.

"Eden, there are worse things than being adopted—" Toomey began.

"Is that so?" she interrupted, her sarcasm still intact.

He came closer, perhaps to offer her the shoulder she had wanted earlier. "Maybe you'll be able to locate your natural mother—"

"My 'natural' mother can't be identified. Whatever that means. What am I going to do?" she said, still pacing. "I never expected— I *never*— I can't deal with this."

"Eden—"

"You don't understand!"

"Then help me out here."

"Edna never would talk about my father. Never. But I always thought he was a lawyer friend of hers who used to come out to the digs to see her. He was the only man I ever remember her being even remotely interested in, and he was always kind to me. So I thought it had to be him. She always said that marriage was all wrong for her—I thought maybe they'd been married for a little while and then divorced. Or maybe she heard her biological clock ticking and he helped her out without making it legal. But I was wrong. The lawyer wasn't my father at all. My father was some—my father was a Navajo—"

Toomey stood looking at her—as if he were still waiting for the punch line.

"No kidding," he said finally. "So was mine."

"You don't understand," she said again.

"Oh, sure I do. I tell you what. You keep it on the QT—*I'm* certainly not going to tell anybody—and maybe you won't have your country club membership canceled. Like I said, Ms. Trevoy—have a nice life."

Chapter Five

Toomey decided on the drive back to Window Rock that there was a great deal of truth in that old bromide Ignorance Is Bliss. He was certainly a lot more blissful when he was completely in the dark about Professor Trevoy and her daughter. And now the more he learned, the more out of harmony he became.

Eden Trevoy was wrong. He did understand. It wasn't difficult to grasp at all. Until that trip into the arroyo, she had been a poor-little-misunderstood-and-neglected rich girl. Now she was the illegitimate child of an unknown white woman and a Navajo man. He had no doubt that her birth mother had been white. She had to have been, because Eden looked white in spite of her dark hair and eyes. A little on the exotic side, maybe—now that he knew her family tree—but white nonetheless.

Now what? he kept thinking. And he was still thinking it when he pulled into the law enforcement building parking lot. He got out of the vehicle, but he didn't go immediately inside. He stood looking up at the sky overhead, then at the horizon, then turning his face into the wind. After a moment he realized he wasn't alone. A woman stood nearby watching him.

"Mrs. Singer—" he said, recognizing her and trying not to appear as startled as he was.

"Officer Toomey," the lieutenant's wife said.

But she didn't say anything else, and she didn't go away, either. He stood there, waiting, because it was the polite thing to do.

"Can I help you with anything?" he asked finally, because he knew her well enough to do that. She came to the police station to see Lucas often—sometimes at Mary Skeets's urging to drag the lieutenant out to lunch or supper or whatever, when he—and therefore everyone else in the building—was having a particularly bad day.

"I was about to ask you that," she said.

"Me?" he asked.

"I know the look, Ben," she said.

"The look?"

"The tribal-cop-out-of-harmony one."

"No, no, I'm fine," he assured her. He smiled so she could see how fine he was.

"Lucas is strict, but you can talk to him, you know."

He didn't say anything. He glanced in her direction. She had obviously come here directly from her job at the medical clinic. She still had on her lab coat; every pocket had something—a lot of things—crammed into it. Nurses were apparently like tribal cops. They needed a lot of paraphernalia to function.

She kept looking at him. Sloan Singer was an attractive woman, he thought. And he thought she was kind. The People called her Smiles-at-Children, and she certainly hadn't blamed him for his part in the marriage of Lucas's sister to Captain Becenti. In fact, he had the distinct impression that Mrs. Singer had been very pleased about it. He knew that she had come to the rez maybe twenty years ago, a white woman looking for a lost brother or something. And she had married Lucas Singer and stayed. He didn't doubt that she would recognize the tribal-cop-out-of-harmony look, just as he didn't doubt that he himself had it. How could he help but have it?

"I...it's not a tribal police thing," he finally offered. "It's nothing to worry the lieutenant with."

"It was very sad about the one who died," she said, startling him even more. Part of him was astounded that she was astute enough to make the leap to Edna Trevoy, and part of him appreciated her respect she showed for him by not mentioning the dead person's name.

She suddenly smiled. "I'm not psychic, Ben. I'm logical. Mary Skeets told me you'd gone to the memorial service. And I heard about you looking for the professor when she was missing. It was all very...strange."

He gave a quiet sigh. She was still looking at him, and he realized that the door was wide open. Here was a person who could perhaps give him some insight. He could say what was on his mind right now if he wanted to. He could tell her. He *would* tell her.

"I don't understand white people," he said—which was and wasn't the crux of the problem.

"The one who died, you mean?"

"Yes," he said, and suddenly he was telling her the whole story from that first call to the police station straight through to the letter and Eden Trevoy's reaction to it.

"I'm thinking the best thing I can do now is—nothing," he finished. "I don't have the letter anymore. I'm done with it."

He glanced at Mrs. Singer. She had a slight frown.

"What?" he asked. "You don't think I'm done with it?"

The front doors of the law enforcement building opened. Lucas Singer came walking out.

Great, Toomey thought. Lucas was going to know exactly what time Toomey got back from the memorial service. Among other things.

But he found suddenly that he didn't care if Lucas found out about Edna Trevoy's letter. He wasn't about to try to swear Mrs. Singer to secrecy. He just wanted her opinion.

"What I think," Mrs. Singer said, giving her husband a wave, "is that this all depends on how satisfied you are with the reason."

"What reason?"

"The reason the one who died did all this."

"I don't know the reason."

"Well, there you are then," she said.

"There I am?"

"If you need to know the reason—even if it makes sense only to the one who died—then you aren't done. You see?" She smiled again and went to meet her husband.

Exactly, Toomey thought, watching as Lucas opened the car door for her. I'm not done.

But he wasn't certain in what way he wasn't done. Yes, he had an overwhelming sense of business unfinished. No, he didn't have any idea how or where he should begin to finish it. Or even if he should finish it.

When in doubt, wait, he finally decided. The ball was definitely not in his court. And if he waited long enough, perhaps the need to know would dissipate. The one who died had said she had wanted to "tie up loose ends." There was a lot to be said for tidying up life's little messes.

He went inside the law enforcement building. Mary Skeets was waiting for him like the proverbial spider waiting for the fly—only it was curiosity that drove her, not the need for prey. And she wasn't all that curious about the memorial service. She was more interested in why he had been talking to Mrs. Singer in the parking lot.

"Lucas was surprised," she said.

"Yeah? What did he say?"

"He didn't *say* anything."

"Then how do you know he was surprised?"

"Because there was more to the conversation than 'Hello, how are you?' and because I've been working with him since he was a baby patrolman like you. So what were you and Sloan talking about?"

"Mary—" he said in exasperation. "This is really *not* your business."

"Right," she agreed. "So what were you talking about?"

"I just wanted her opinion about something, okay?"

"Like what?"

"Like…white people."

"You asked her for her opinion about white people."

"Yeah."

"And she told you."

"Yeah," he said again.

"Benjamin, sometimes I think all those haircuts your sister has given you have done something to your brain," she said, going back to her phones.

Maybe so, he thought as he walked to his desk and sat down. But talking to Mrs. Singer had helped him to get a better focus on the problem. The problem was that he didn't know the reason for anything. *That* was the problem.

And, of course, there was Eden Trevoy. And the way she looked and smelled and walked and talked. And the fact that he was spending an inordinate amount of time wondering how she tasted.

And then there was her obvious distress at learning she was half Navajo.

He, on the other hand, wasn't distressed by the revelation at all. In fact, he was pleased. Very pleased. She was still unreachable—but not nearly so far beyond his grasp as she had been when he had left for Gallup earlier.

Even so, there was nothing to be done. Yet.

What could the reason be? he thought, drumming his fingers on the desktop. What?

"Toomey!"

He jumped violently, just as the lieutenant had intended.

"Sir!" he responded, as if he had been paying a lot more attention than it may have appeared.

"Don't you have anything to do?"

"Yes, sir!" he answered.

"Too much to do?" Lucas asked.

"No, sir!"

"Good. Come into my office."

Lucas Singer intended that Toomey stay busy, *much* busier than he himself would have elected to be if he had had any choice about it—which he didn't. Coyote, the metaphysical mischief maker of the Navajo, had run amok on the reservation. A rash of freak accidents, nonelective surgeries and acute illnesses had befallen enough tribal police officers to leave both the Chinle and Crown Point substations seriously undermanned. At the same time there was a sharp increase in bootlegging activities, petty larceny and domestic violence in both areas. Toomey was immediately volunteered to help stem the tide, running back and forth between Chinle and Crown Point—which was no small trip.

"Lucas and Becenti must think I've got a plane," he complained to Mary Skeets when he dropped off some papers on his way from one substation to the other. Again.

"Oh, quit whining," she said. "It could be worse."

"I don't see how. You know how many trips I've made in the last two weeks? It can't be cost effective."

"You could be on horseback—or walking. That's pretty cost effective."

"Oh, thanks, Mary," he said. "Now I've really got something to worry about."

She laughed and shooed him away.

"Toomey!" Lucas yelled as he was about to go out the door.

"Stayed too long, Benjamin," Mary sang under her breath—a split second before Lucas reached him.

"Let's go," Lucas said.

"Sir?"

"I'm going to Crown Point with you. I need to check on something there and there's no reason to take two vehicles—and, please, try to look a little more delighted. You're going to hurt my feelings."

"Oh, I'm delighted, sir," Toomey said, opening the front door for him and not daring to even glance in Mary's direction. "Really."

All the way across the parking lot, he tried to remember what condition the inside of the police vehicle was in. His mind was completely blank. Generally speaking, he was a reasonably neat person. No clutter. No used fast-food wrappers or boxes. He earnestly hoped that he had continued in this vein, but he couldn't be sure. During the long back-and-forth trips, he'd had his mind on other things. No, he'd had his mind on one thing.

Eden Trevoy.

He opened the door on the driver's side, silently rejoicing that there was absolutely nothing on the front passenger seat. He got in and unlocked the door for Lucas. This was going to be a whole lot like the time he had to drive Captain Becenti all the way to Santa Fe in a snowstorm *and* testify in a federal trial—only worse.

Lucas climbed into the vehicle. He wasn't saying anything—but he was looking. And he wasn't being subtle about it. He had several folders in his hand and he stuck them down between the seats.

"What's this?" he asked when he got the folders tangled in a black cord.

"It's a—ah...DC to DC adaptor, sir," Toomey said, mentally kicking himself because he had forgotten all about the jerry rigging.

"And it's hooked to?" Lucas asked, even though he could clearly see the answer.

"Cigarette lighter, sir."

"The other end, Toomey."

"That would be a boom box, sir," Toomey said.

"Why?"

"Why?"

"That's the question, Toomey. Why?"

"To listen to music, sir—cassette tapes—when I'm driving back and forth. It saves on batteries," he added.

"It saves *you* on batteries. I'm not sure what it does for the law enforcement budget. How permanent is this thing?"

"It's not, sir. Permanent, that is. I used alligator clips on the other end—clipped to the positive and negative terminals—and you just unplug the other end from the cigarette lighter."

"How come you know how to do all that?"

"It was a long time before we got electricity out our way, sir. We still wouldn't have it if it wasn't windy

enough for one of those big wind generators. I had to make
do with the truck battery.''

"So let's hear it.''

"Hear it, sir?''

"Yes, Toomey. I want to hear it.''

"I doubt if I've got any music you'd like—''

"You let me decide, okay?''

Toomey gave up and punched the cassette Play button.
The inside of the vehicle immediately filled with his personal favorite—loud, hard-driving, classic rock and roll.

"Let's go,'' Lucas said, and Toomey reached to put an
end to Mick Jagger and his honky-tonk woman.

"No, leave it,'' Lucas said. "I like the Stones.''

Eden arrived in Window Rock in the late afternoon. She
drove directly to the law enforcement building, determined
to do this thing before she lost her nerve. She had spent a
lot of time agonizing about the wisdom of coming back
here, but the plain and simple fact of the matter was that
she was ashamed of herself, and if she was going to feel
better, it would necessitate seeing Ben Toomey. She had
hoped that he might come to see her—or at least telephone—but he hadn't. And after two weeks, it was apparent to her that she was going to have to take care of this
herself.

She parked in the parking lot and went immediately inside the building. The place was much less crowded than
it had been at her last visit. She went directly to the woman
manning the phones and stood waiting for her to look up.

"May I help you?'' the woman asked almost immediately.

"I'd like to see Officer Ben Toomey—if he's here.''

"You just missed him,'' she said. "I expect he's gone
home—but I'm not sure.''

"Oh. Well—"

"Just a minute," the woman said, holding up her hand. "Lieutenant Singer," she called to someone behind Eden. "Do you know if Ben Toomey went back to Chinle or if he was going home?"

"He went home. Why?"

"She's looking for him," the woman said, nodding in Eden's direction.

"Why?" the lieutenant asked as he walked up. The question was for Eden.

He was obviously in charge, and he was obviously trying to assess what she was doing here—again. She had no doubt that he recognized her from her previous visit.

But she had never been one to be intimidated by people in authority. It was something she had learned very early on—at a very prestigious Eastern boarding school.

"Does he live far from here?" she asked, ignoring the question.

"I asked why you want to see him," the lieutenant said, apparently because he wasn't one to be intimidated, either.

"It's personal," she said. Period.

"Personal," he repeated. "There seems to be a lot of that going around lately. Don't let it get in the way of tribal police business."

He looked at her for a long moment, then walked away.

Eden stared after him, frowning. Even if he had recognized her from the last time she was here, she didn't deserve *that*. She understood him completely. Public facility or not, Eden Trevoy was *not* welcome here.

She turned back to the woman in charge of the phones.

"Does Ben live far from here?" she asked.

"Not too far—but it's kind of complicated."

"Could you give me directions?"

The woman hesitated. "You're not going to jump all over him again, are you?"

Eden gave a quiet sigh. "No," she said. "I'm not. Actually, I was planning on apologizing. For the second time."

"Good," the woman said. "Because he's had kind of a rough day. Let me get this phone call and then I'll write the directions down for you."

Eden stood waiting. "Is the other officer—the lieutenant—always this—" She stopped, because she couldn't think of a word that wouldn't be presumptuous. And one person ready to show her the door was enough.

"Yes," the woman said, smiling. "But it's not that he's being rude. It's that he cares about his officers. Keeps up with them, you know? It's kind of a Navajo thing. You have to keep everything in balance, your job and your private life, or nothing works. So anything the lieutenant thinks might not be good for an officer's harmony—well…"

Eden got the picture. Her first visit to the law enforcement building aside, this Lieutenant Singer had decided that she would not be good for Ben Toomey.

The woman handed her the piece of paper she'd been writing on, then went over the somewhat complicated directions.

"It's only about ten miles," she said.

"Ten?" Eden said, looking down at the convoluted map.

"As the crow flies," the woman amended. "When you see Ben," she added when Eden looked up, "I wouldn't mention your conversation with the lieutenant."

"Why not?"

"Like I said. He's had kind of a rough day."

The map turned out to be very accurate, and it took Eden

much less time than she had anticipated to find the place where Ben Toomey lived. The shadows were long when she drove down the rutted road to his front door, but there was still plenty of daylight.

She had stopped questioning whether or not she was doing the sensible thing. Edna Trevoy, for all her faults, had not brought her adopted daughter up to be a bigot—under any circumstances. Eden had been insensitive and insulting, and she was going to tell Ben Toomey that she regretted her behavior. Then she was going to get into her car and drive straight back to Albuquerque. Her conscience would be eased, and that, as they say, would be that.

She pulled into the dusty yard and stopped. There were several other cars and trucks around, including the white sports-utility vehicle that belonged to the tribal police. This had to be the place, she thought, and there was nothing left for her to do at this point but get out.

She walked toward the trailer, but she didn't see anyone. She could hear loud music coming from around back—some kind of bluesy rock and roll song about the good dying young. She walked in that direction. She could smell something cooking—meat on a charcoal grill, she realized as she rounded the corner. She realized, too, that there was a reason for all those vehicles. Ben Toomey was having some kind of high-spirited party—and she had just crashed it. All conversation abruptly stopped when she appeared, and all heads turned in her direction.

"Hi," she said over the music—because there wasn't much else she could do. "I'm looking for Ben Toomey."

"He's inside," one of the young men said, looking at her appreciatively. "Ben!" he yelled into the nearest window. "Somebody here to see you!"

"Yeah, okay!" she heard him answer.

In a moment someone came around the side of the

trailer, but it wasn't Ben. It was a very pretty young woman carrying a platter filled with a lot of food. She also had a lot of bosom and a lot of shapely leg showing, and she put the platter on the picnic table in a way that suggested she was very proud of all three abundances. Eden wondered, perhaps not so idly, what exactly this girl was to Ben Toomey.

Girlfriend, she decided abruptly. Maybe more.

Eden looked at the trailer window, but she couldn't see anyone. Of course, Toomey would be surprised to find her here. She was surprised herself. She could hear a police scanner noisily monitoring official radio traffic inside the trailer, and water running, and then a cabinet door closing. She glanced at Toomey's guests. One of the girls—not the busty, leggy one—stood.

"Hi," the girl said finally, walking closer. "I'm Ben's sister, Faye. I *love* your hair. Do you mind if I look?"

"Look?" Eden asked, a bit startled.

"I'm going to beauty school. Could I just see how it's cut?"

"Oh, sure," Eden said, standing still for the inspection.

"I think I could do that," Faye said as she ran her fingers through Eden's hair.

Everyone else burst into laughter.

"I could!" Faye insisted. "I can see exactly how it's done. It's layered just a little and these ends here are—"

"If I were you, Eden, I'd run for my life," Ben said behind them, making everyone laugh again.

"Oh, you're really cute, Ben," Faye said. "One of these days—when I'm rich and famous—you're going to call me on the phone and *beg* me to cut your hair. And I'm going to say Ben *who?*"

He laughed good-naturedly and turned to Eden. "Did you meet everybody?"

"Ah...no," Eden said. "Just your sister."

He introduced her to the rest of the group—a gracious thing for him to do, she thought, given the way they had parted. She noted that the men were all members of the Navajo Tribal Police, but she still didn't know the relationship busty Angel—no, Angelina—had with Ben.

"So how did you get way out here?" he asked Eden when the introductions were over.

"A woman at the law enforcement building—I guess she's the dispatcher. She drew me a map," she said, trying to look more at ease than she felt. She hadn't planned to do this with an audience.

"Mary Skeets?"

"I don't know. We didn't do the name thing."

"If you didn't, it's because she already knows yours."

"Oh, I don't think so."

"You don't know Mary Skeets. What she doesn't know, she finds out."

They stood awkwardly.

"So *why* did you get way out here?" Ben asked, because it was the only question left.

"Not to crash your party," she said, walking away from the group. He walked with her.

"It's not a party," he said. "It's more a cheer-old-Ben-up kind of thing."

"Yes, I heard you had a bad day."

"Not bad, exactly. Stressful. I had to drive my lieutenant to Crown Point and back. It was...an experience."

Singer? she almost asked, but then she would have had to say how she knew him.

"You have good friends—to do that for you," she said instead.

"Yeah, I do. So," he said. He let his eyes meet hers. "Can you stay? We're about to eat here—"

"No," she interrupted. "I just came to apologize. *Again,*" she admitted, glancing at him. He looked different out of uniform, and he *was* handsome, she decided. T-shirt, jeans, ball cap and all.

Handsome.

He didn't say anything. He was watching her closely as if for some clue as to her real intent. He didn't quite believe the apology premise. She knew that, and she didn't blame him. She took a few more steps away, because she could see Angelina overtly watching them, but he didn't come along with her.

She stopped and looked at him a long moment before she continued.

"I was insulting," she said finally. "And I regret it. You've been nothing but kind to me—and to my—" she broke off and looked away "— my mother," she continued, looking up at him.

He still didn't say anything, and she forced a smile.

"Well—that's it. That's all I came for. I'll go now. Enjoy your...cheering-up party."

"Eden," he said when she was walking away. "How are you? Really."

She didn't answer and she didn't stop.

"Eden—" he said, catching up with her. "What are you going to do?"

"About what?"

"About being half Navajo."

"Nothing," she said, surprised. What could she possibly do about something like that?

"I know it's hard," he said. "You've lost your whole identity. But I've been thinking a lot about this. If you want to try to find out something about who you are, I have an idea."

"What kind of idea?" she asked.

"You don't have any relatives to teach you," he said, and she sighed.

"I don't know what that means, Ben."

"If you're Navajo—even half Navajo—it's important to have relatives to show you things—teach you how to behave and how to live in harmony."

"How to follow the rules, you mean," she said.

"Something like that."

"I had to go to traffic school once. I didn't like it."

"Oh, well, this would be a *lot* worse than that," he assured her. "Since you don't have any relatives, I thought I could loan you one of mine. My grandmother, Sadie."

"To teach me?"

"Yeah."

"How to be Navajo?"

"No. To teach you what being Navajo means. So you know something about your heritage. The way you were brought up, I don't think you could ever *be* Navajo. But you could learn something about your father's people."

"No," she said, walking away again. "There's no point in it."

"Eden—"

"Why should I waste my time on that?" she asked, turning back to him. "*He* certainly never wasted any time on me."

"That doesn't matter. It is not about him. It's about you."

She shook her head and walked on toward her car.

"Think about it," he called after her. "Call me at the law enforcement building if you change your mind. Mary Skeets will get the message to me if I'm not there. Did you hear what I said?"

"No!" she called back. She got into her car and backed around, convinced that Ben Toomey just could *not* leave well enough alone.

Chapter Six

The good news was that Toomey no longer had to drive back and forth between Chinle and Crown Point. The bad news was that he was attached to the Crown Point substation more or less permanently, at least until one of their officers recuperated enough from his fall off a highly vexed horse to come back to work. Toomey understood the dynamics here. He had been both right and wrong to go off looking for the then-missing, now-deceased professor, and as a result, anything the Navajo Tribal Police needed that required significant physical and mental inconvenience had his name on it. He was still on the Lucas Singer version of The List, all right, but he was now at the top.

Actually, Toomey believed that this particular assignment was for the best. If he had stayed in Window Rock, he would have spent an inordinate amount of time waiting to hear from Eden Trevoy. As it was, he called Mary

Skeets several times to see if he had any messages. He didn't really expect that Eden would take him up on his offer, no matter how much sense it made—to him. To her it was obviously a bad solution to an even worse problem. Still, he thought that he and Eden had very similar ways of looking at things. He wasn't happy being in the dark, particularly about matters that directly affected him, but he thought that they both had distinct hide-it-under-a-rug-and-hope-it-goes-away tendencies.

"Ben," Mary Skeets said in exasperation when he telephoned Window Rock yet another time. "The only calls you've gotten have been about the cases you were working on. Joey Nez is taking care of them for you, and he's leaving all the message slips on your desk so you'll know who called when you get back. If you get a *personal* message, I will let you know. Okay?"

He didn't call again.

But hope sprang eternal—Eden was the one who had come to Window Rock to see *him*. Even so, nearly four weeks passed, and, eventually, he had no choice but to return to that same old conclusion. He would do well to forget that he had ever met the late professor's daughter. Their paths had crossed briefly when they were children and again when they were adults. And that was all that could be said of the situation.

To take his mind off this weakly resolved dilemma, he worked long hours, paying particular attention to the Crown Point way of doing things. It was considerably different from the standard operating procedures in Window Rock. He noted for future reference who was supposed to be in charge and who was *really* in charge, who to ask for if he ever needed someone at the Crown Point station to answer a question. And he actually believed that his staying so busy was helping. He actually felt that he was almost over the worst of it—until he was abruptly reassigned again, this time back to Window Rock.

The law enforcement building was busy when he returned, crowded with all sorts of police business and the ensuing upset civilians. Mary was juggling a rash of telephone calls. He didn't wait to ask her if Lucas wanted to see him. He *knew* Lucas wanted to see him, but he went immediately to his own desk instead—such as it was. It was still jammed in the tiny space by the file cabinets, and there were a number of While You Were Out memos scattered over the top of it. He shuffled through them quickly and tossed them aside.

Nothing.

He didn't know why he was surprised. Mary had said she would let him know if he had any personal messages, but as much as it might alert her that he was more than a little interested in Eden Trevoy, he was still going to ask.

Mary was still on the phone when he came out, but she was either listening and not talking, or she was on hold.

"Anything new out your mother's way?" she asked as he walked up.

"New?" he asked, but she immediately turned away from him to talk into the receiver.

What could be new? he thought. New wind generator? New road? New niece or nephew on the way?

"I don't know," he said when he thought she had finished. "I haven't been home in three weeks."

"Oh, yeah, I forgot," she said as the phone rang again.

He waited.

"So have you seen Lucas yet?" she asked, when she realized he was still standing there. She raised and lowered her eyebrows once.

He was in no mood to be teased about his tempestuous relationship with his superior officer. "Mary, did—"

Several people walked up.

"I'm busy, Benjamin," she said. "And you're going to be busy, too, if Lucas sees you standing around out here instead of reporting in."

A good point, he thought, giving up. He wasn't going to ask about Eden with an audience, and he certainly hadn't missed being yelled at. He did *not* want to get on the lieutenant's wrong side the very minute he returned. He sighed wearily and went to advise Lucas that his favorite officer was back in the fold.

"Joey Nez is going to take some vacation time," Lucas said, barely looking up from his paperwork. "You can go by his schedule until Mary gets around to making a new one." He handed it to Toomey and waited while he looked at it.

"Questions?"

"No, sir," Toomey said, but he couldn't help noticing that, according to this calendar, Officer Toomey was standing here in the middle of Lucas Singer's office on his one day off this week.

"Okay, then. That's all."

"Yes, sir."

"Toomey," Lucas said when he was about to open the door. "They tell me you did a good job in Crown Point."

Toomey looked at him, too surprised to respond.

"You interested in going back there?" Lucas asked.

"Do I have a choice, sir?"

"Answer the question, Toomey. Are you interested in going to Crown Point on a permanent basis or not?"

"I'd rather stay here in Window Rock if I can, sir."

"Why?"

"Because I'm the only son left here, sir. It's hard on the family—my mother and my grandmother—if I'm not close enough to help out."

Lucas didn't say anything, and Toomey stood there wondering what this was all about. He actually thought that the lieutenant didn't believe him—when Lucas Singer knew Toomey's family situation. He knew that two of Toomey's brothers lived off the rez now and that the one who had joined the army had come back from a Middle East "police action" in a metal box. And yet, Toomey had the distinct impression that he was being given some kind of test, one in which only Lucas Singer had the No. 2 pencil.

"Okay, that's all," Lucas said abruptly.

Toomey hesitated. "Am I going back to Crown Point, sir?" he dared to ask.

"I haven't decided."

He hasn't decided, Toomey thought as he stepped into the hall. Lucas Singer's standard reply when he had no intention of answering the question. The drive to Crown Point with the lieutenant had been a revelation to Toomey—who would have thought the man liked the Rolling Stones? But Lucas was rapidly becoming like everything else in Toomey's life of late. The more he knew, the less he understood.

He made a copy of Joey Nez's schedule, taped the original to his desk and gave the copy to the still-very-busy Mary Skeets.

"Have you seen the Trevoy girl?" she asked when he turned to go.

"What do you mean?" he asked.

"Benjamin, I can't get any plainer than that. Have you seen the Trevoy girl? She came in here asking for you several times while you were in Crown Point."

"I thought you were going to let me know if I had any messages!" he said in exasperation.

"And I would have—if she'd left one. She didn't."

"Well, what did she say?"

"Um, let's see. Something like, 'Is Officer Toomey in today?' Or, 'Is Officer Toomey back from Crown Point?'"

"That's it?"

"That's it."

"She didn't say where she'd be or how I could get in touch with her?"

"None of the above," Mary assured him. "Do you know if—" She broke off and shook her head. "Never mind," she said.

"What, Mary? Do I know if what?"

"She hasn't had some kind of run-in with Lucas, has she?"

"Lucas? No. Not that I know of. Why?"

"I just wondered. He's not crazy about her coming in here. He asked her again exactly what she wanted with you."

"Again? What do mean 'again'?"

"The first time she told him it was personal. This last time she said she needed to see you regarding her mother's death."

"What did Lucas say to her?"

"Nothing really—but he didn't like either answer."

Toomey left, considerably more depressed than when he had arrived. He went to the grocery store and bought several food items he couldn't afford. Then he drove home to his trailer, fully expecting to find something wrong there. Ever since he'd gone on that quest to locate the late professor, his already precarious optimism had all but failed him.

But everything about the place seemed to be in order. Nothing flooded or broken or burned. No appliances run amok. His sister Faye had even remembered to come over and empty out the refrigerator and take the perishables to the rest of the family.

He finished putting the groceries away, and he decided that he needed to run. He changed into shorts and running shoes. He'd been cooped up too long, and he needed to think about this latest development regarding the late professor's daughter—and what he intended to do about it. The terrain was rugged enough to give him a good workout, but not complicated enough to keep him from thinking. He would completely immerse himself in the intricacies of the problem and see what turned up.

And something did turn up, but certainly not what he expected. When he finished his run and returned to the trailer, Eden Trevoy was sitting quietly on the bottom step.

"What are you doing here?" he asked bluntly, startling her with his sudden appearance. He hadn't decided much during his fit of physical exertion, but he did know he was tired of second-guessing.

He tried not to stare at her. Her hair was still fashionably in her eyes and she was wearing a short pink-flowered dress that showed off her bare, tanned legs to their best advantage. She looked crisp and cool and untouchable— and amazingly smooth and soft and inviting, all at the same time. And she smelled so good. He, on the other hand, was out of breath and hot and sweaty, the ultimate in rank, less-than-dainty males. He deliberately sat down on the steps close to her.

"Mary Skeets told me you were back," she said.

"I repeat. What are you doing here?"

"Following Navajo decorum, I thought," she said. "As I understand it, I don't go pounding on the door. I wait for you to come out."

"Well, that only works if I'm inside and I know you're out here," he said. He reached for the towel he'd left on the steps and wiped his sweaty face and belly. "How long have you been waiting?"

"Not long. Well, long enough to change my mind several times."

"About what?"

"About whether or not I want to take you up on your offer—if you haven't changed *your* mind."

"So what's the verdict? The latest verdict," he qualified.

"The verdict is that you're probably right. I probably do need to find out more—about who I really am."

"You just woke up one morning and decided I was right," he said.

"Well, there was a little more to it than that."

"Yeah? Like what?"

"Like lunch," she said.

"Lunch?"

"In Albuquerque. With some of my old college friends. We went to Étienne's a few weeks ago. It's a—"

"I know what it is," he said. And he did. Just as he knew he would have to take out a second mortgage on his vintage trailer to ever eat there.

"When I left here the other day, I was absolutely certain that I didn't want to go on any kind of a cultural quest. But then, in the restaurant, with these women—my *friends*—I—" She stopped and looked off into the distance. "I suddenly realized that all of them have the same career goal," she said after a moment.

"Which is?"

"To divorce well."

It occurred to him suddenly how little he knew about her. She could have the same goal, for all he knew. She could already be engaged. Or married and halfway there.

"One of them had a brother who had been arrested—for 'bashing' someone," she said, still looking elsewhere.

"Bashing who?" he asked, because he immediately understood that there was something she wasn't saying.

She looked at him. "A...man who'd been drinking. He'd passed out in this park. He was lying on the ground and her brother and these other boys beat him up."

"A drunk Indian, you mean?"

He saw the flicker of surprise in her eyes. She hadn't expected that he would be so astute. She had a lot to learn. About the so-called "Indian problem" and about him.

"Yes," she said.

"It's considered great sport in some circles," he said, draping the towel around his neck.

"They hurt him really badly. And she was all incensed—not because of what her brother did, but because he'd been arrested and the case was actually going to court. I looked around the table and I thought, 'What am I doing here?'"

"Yeah, well, having your consciousness raised can be a very painful procedure."

"No, it wasn't that. You have to *have* consciousness before anybody can raise it. I...thought maybe I ought to come see if I could get some."

She was looking into his eyes now, searching for whatever answer she must think he had. He held her gaze as long as he could. He was rapidly losing the battle to keep her at a safe distance. She kept surprising him with her candor. And, of course, there was the way she looked.

"Do you have to get back to Albuquerque right away or anything?" he asked abruptly.

"No. I had some vacation days I had to take or lose. Nearly a month."

"We'll go then," he said, standing up.

She looked up at him. "Where are we going?"

"To see the head of the family. My grandmother, Sadie Benally."

She smiled, a real smile that lit up her face and eyes. "Now there's something I really like about the Navajo."

"What's that?"

"Women are the boss."

He tried not to smile in return and didn't quite make it. "Can you walk in those shoes?"

"Of course—what's wrong with them?"

"Oh, nothing," he assured her. "You just don't see many people hiking on the rez in lace-up, canvas platforms with lug soles."

"I can walk in them," she insisted. She flashed that smile again. "The traction is truly remarkable."

"I'll bet. Okay. You just remember I asked. Do you want something to drink before we go?" he asked.

"No, thank you."

"I'm going to get something—and shower and change clothes. If you're still here when I come out..."

"I'll be here," she assured him.

He knew exactly what he was doing by suggesting that they go on foot. He wanted a memory, one he could keep always, one of being with her here, now, in the place that meant more to him than he could have ever explained. Mother Earth. Father Sky. Eden Trevoy.

He didn't take her by the road, which would have been longer but less adventuresome, given her choice of footwear. He took her through the red rock monoliths. And he would have to say that she hadn't lied. She could walk in those shoes of hers just fine.

"We aren't going to get lost, are we?" she asked as they threaded their way along the winding and sometimes treacherous foot path that only he could see.

"Well, nothing's impossible," he said over his shoulder. "But it would be a first. No Toomey in living memory has ever gotten lost going to his grandma's house."

"Are there any snakes around here?"

"What are you worried about? I'm the one in front."

She laughed, stumbled over her lug soles and grabbed the back of his shirt to keep from falling. He had to keep reminding himself that he was letting his expectations get way, *way* ahead of his reality. Half Navajo or not, this was still Eden Trevoy, the poor little rich girl, hanging on to him for dear life so she could make it up the sharp and narrow incline without getting snakebit.

Eventually the path widened and the land grew flat. She let go of his shirt. He could see the family compound in the distance. He tried to look at it through her eyes. To him it was home. To her it must be primitive beyond belief.

She looked much more mussed up and touchable by the time they reached the front yard of his mother's small rectangular house, and he had to keep reminding himself that it was futile to let his mind go wandering off into some wild sexual fantasy. They were here for a reason, and that reason had very little to do with him.

They were greeted only by the dogs. No one came out of the house when he called, and he didn't see his mother or his grandmother around the corrals or the sheep pens. The family's traditional mud and log hogan stood apart from everything else, off to one side.

"Wait here," he said to Eden, and he walked in that direction, the dogs still bouncing around his legs.

The hogan was empty, as well. So was the "shade" house made of cut saplings where the family congregated for meals and cooking during the summer. He walked the short distance out to his grandmother Sadie's house—a hexagon-shaped structure like the traditional hogan, but made with lumber and vinyl siding instead. It also had three, very fine roll-out windows—a great source of pride to Grandma Sadie. He peered into one of them. No one was at home.

He gave a loud whistle, which stirred up the dogs again, and he randomly patted their heads to keep them from jumping all over him. The truck was parked in its usual place, so the family must be somewhere close.

"Hey!" someone said, and he turned sharply around. His sister Faye stood on the other side of the corral fence, grinning. "Look what the coyotes dragged up."

"Where is everybody?" he asked, walking closer.

"Here and there," she answered vaguely. "I'm not exactly sure."

"What do you mean, you're not exactly sure?"

"Something scattered the sheep. Mom and Grandma went looking for them. They've been gone a long time. It's hard telling where they are at this point."

"They went without the dogs?"

"Grandma took *her* dog. The rest of them don't know a sheep from a kangaroo."

He frowned. "How come you're not in school?"

"It's Saturday, Ben. You know, the weekend?"

"Yeah, I've heard of it," he said. "But not lately."

"Poor Benjy. Have the mean old Tribal Police been treating you bad?"

He ignored the sisterly sarcasm. "I've brought someone with me," he said.

"Who?"

"Eden Trevoy."

"That girl that came by your place the other day?"

"Yeah," he said.

"She finally found you, I guess," Faye said, and he frowned again.

"*Everybody* knows she's been looking for you, Benjamin," she said pointedly. "What everybody doesn't know is *why?*"

"She needs help with a personal problem," he said. "I think Grandma Sadie can help her."

Faye looked at him for a moment. "Maybe so. You know, I kind of liked her—she's got great hair. I don't think Mom will like her, though."

"Why not?"

"Because of you, silly."

"Me?"

"Yes, you. You know how our mother feels about forward women. She knows Eden *and* Angelina came out to your place to see you—on the same day, too."

"Yeah, and I wonder how she knows that?"

Faye grinned and gave him an arch look. "It's not like it's a secret, Benjy. Joey Nez was *really* impressed—two women running after you like that. Angelina wasn't exactly thrilled that Eden showed up, though. You got anything going with her?"

"Who?"

"Angelina! Will you pay attention? Well, Eden, too, for that matter."

"No and no," he assured her.

"Mom will be very happy to hear that. She still thinks you live by yourself so you can have this really wild sex life."

He laughed. On a scale of ten, his sex life would have had to be rated in minus numbers. It occurred to him, too, that in the not too distant past, he had earnestly intended to improve those numbers with the fetching Angelina.

He looked around as the dogs cut loose again in a frenzy

of barking. He could see his mother and grandmother approaching the compound on horseback—without the sheep, it appeared.

"Go tell them I've brought a visitor, will you?" he said to Faye.

"I'm busy, Ben. You do it."

"Faye, I need a minute to make sure Eden understands a few things. Help me out here."

His sister sighed, but offered no further argument.

"Hey, Ben?" she called after him. "You know you could use a haircut."

"In your dreams, kid," he said, making her laugh.

Eden was still waiting where he left her, one of the considerably less vigilant watchdogs sprawled at her feet. Once again he was struck by how pretty she was. He was struck, too, by the fact that, unlike the rich girls he had encountered at the university, she didn't seem to be quite so flagrantly aware of it.

"A couple of things," he said to her as he approached. "When you talk to my grandmother, try not to look at her too directly. It's not polite. Okay?"

"Okay," she said.

"And the conversation isn't going to be what you're used to. It's going to be full of long silences—but don't let that worry you. It's just the way it's done. And don't mention the name of the one who died."

She gave a quiet sigh.

"You're...okay with this?" he asked.

She nodded.

"What will you tell her—about me?" she asked.

"Everything I know," he said. "Why?"

"I just wondered." The dog rolled over onto her foot, and she pulled it free and walked away a few steps. She stood looking at the monoliths in the distance. "It's not just a whim," she said, looking back at him. "My doing this."

"I didn't think it was," he said truthfully, regardless of how he may have sounded earlier. She had been trying to find him, according to Faye and to Mary Skeets. She had come all the way out to his place today specifically to tell him that she wanted to take him up on his offer of help. It didn't sound like a whim to him.

"I'm going to go help with the horses," he said.

"Do I come or stay?"

"You stay here. Let me do the groundwork."

"This isn't going to cause you any kind of problem, is it?"

"No. No problem. It's just a little…unusual, so I want to give my grandmother time to see how she feels about it. Here comes Faye," he said. "She'll keep you company. I'm pretty sure she's not packing scissors."

Eden gave a soft laugh. "Okay," she said. "I'll wait here."

He needn't have worried about his grandmother. It was his mother who had all the questions. He could tell by the expression on her face that she was more concerned about the young woman he had brought here than about the missing sheep. But he began, anyway, giving his presentation of the recent events in Eden Trevoy's life, the revelation of her adoption and her Navajo father.

"But why did you bring this girl *here*?" his mother asked as soon as he had finished.

"She has no relatives to teach her," he answered.

"Yes," his mother said. Period. Given Faye's report, it was all too apparent to her that Eden Trevoy didn't know how to behave.

"It was my idea that she come," he said. "I thought she could learn something about the Navajo Way from us.

My mother, you knew her when she was a little girl and you knew the one who died. She needs help with this.''

His mother made no reply. He couldn't tell if she thought having known Eden before was a good thing or not.

He waited—he could feel his grandmother waiting, as well—but his mother apparently had nothing more to say.

''She should have been raised by the tribe,'' his grandmother said. ''How is it that she was taken away?''

''I think only the one who died knew the answer to that,'' he said. ''And she never said. When I went into the arroyo to find her, she gave me a letter to keep for Eden. The letter said Eden Trevoy had a Navajo father. That was the first and only information she was ever given.''

''Bring her to my house,'' his grandmother said.

''How do you know this girl isn't writing some kind of paper for school?'' his mother said, apparently not through talking after all.

''She doesn't go to school,'' he said.

''What does she do then?''

''I don't know. Grandma can ask her.''

''Maybe she wants to laugh at us,'' his mother persisted.

''Then she would be laughing at herself, wouldn't she? She comes from what we are.''

''Bring her to my house,'' his grandmother said again.

His mother didn't protest again, but it was clear to him that she wanted to. She looked at him for a moment, then turned and walked away—in a direction that would take her away from where Eden stood waiting.

He sighed.

''She's worried,'' his grandmother said behind him.

''There's nothing for her to worry about.''

''She thinks maybe you'll want to keep this young woman.''

"Nothing."

"Just what do you know about this young woman, Benjamin?"

"I've told you what I know, Mom."

"Everything?"

"Yes," he assured her—except for those things he didn't admit even to himself.

The waiting continued.

"Maybe you should go see," his mother suggested.

"Maybe Faye should go see," he said. "I was invited to take myself elsewhere and not come back until somebody called me. In no uncertain terms."

His mother sighed. Both of them knew Faye was not a good choice for reconnaissance.

But the meeting had apparently ended. His grandmother appeared at the door—alone.

"Are you ready, Benjamin?" she asked. "I'm going to drive you and Eden back to your place."

He was more than ready. He walked with her out to the battered reservation truck where Eden stood waiting, happy to let his grandmother drive because it meant that he would be able to give all his attention to Eden. It was too dark to really see her face. He had a thousand questions, and no one was volunteering anything.

"How did it go?" he asked her as he opened the truck door so she could get in.

"Good," she said.

End of discussion.

They rode the short distance to his place in silence, her leg pressed firmly against his in the dark. He tried to talk to her again when they arrived at his trailer, but she slipped past him and ran to her car, giving him a small wave as she opened the car door. She backed the car around and immediately drove away.

"Benjamin," his grandmother said.

He kept staring after Eden.

"Benjamin," she said again.

He looked in her direction.

"Come around here so I can talk to you."

He went around to the driver's side.

"Eden Trevoy is going to stay with me for a while," she said.

"Stay?"

"It's the only way for her to really learn. She has to stay. She can't learn anything from a few visits or from a book."

He didn't say anything. He was too pleased with this sudden development to comment.

"Benjamin," his grandmother said yet another time. "Are you listening?"

"I'm listening," he said.

"I think your mother is right to worry. I think you already want to keep this young woman."

"Grandma—"

She held up her hand. "It's too much for her—trying to find out who and what she is and having to worry about you, too."

"She doesn't have to worry about me—"

"Benjamin, you've got your police work to do. You tend to that and you let Eden Trevoy learn what she needs to learn. And you don't get in the way."

Chapter Seven

She kept expecting to see him. Every day. And somehow his nonappearance was much more of a distraction than his being here would have been. She surreptitiously watched his family, trying to see if they were in any way affected by his absence. As far as she could tell, *she* was the only one who missed him. Eden could only assume that her taking up residence must be the reason for his staying away, that her being here apparently was an intrusion he just didn't want to have to deal with. For days she had vacillated between being annoyed by his sudden lack of interest and being...hurt. If he hadn't wanted her here, he shouldn't have offered to help her, and he should have objected when his grandmother extended the invitation to stay. She wasn't used to being so blatantly ignored by a man she found...appealing. She was only used to being ignored by real and not-so-real parents.

Or maybe she wasn't the reason for Ben's absence at

all. Maybe he was simply too busy with his job and with Angelina to be making the family rounds. Thus far Eden had resisted the temptation to ask Faye about his girlfriends. There was just enough of the old arrogant Eden Trevoy left to keep her from trying to finagle information about his love life. She had never found herself in the position of being the aggressor before. It was unsettling, particularly when she was certain that she didn't like him all that much in the first place.

She just wanted to talk to him. She desperately needed someone to talk to, someone who at least had some notion of how difficult all this was. She was so alone now, and in a way she wouldn't have been if the always-tenuous tie between her and Edna hadn't been broken. She had discovered the huge difference in being solitary by choice and being lonely. She walked around all the time wanting to weep and yet she absolutely refused to give in to it. No more useless tears, she had decided when she was still a child, and she had meant it.

She was adjusting physically to the Toomey-Benally lifestyle. After a few days she was able to get up at what Sadie optimistically referred to as "first light" without falling dead asleep by mid-afternoon. She had no problem with the food. In fact, she rather liked most of it. But emotionally and intellectually, she was at a complete loss. Today, Sadie was "listening" to plants, and while she listened, Eden followed carefully in her footsteps from one patch of wild growth to another, trying to learn the things Sadie wanted to teach her, trying not to think about Sadie's policeman grandson. She and Sadie had been out all day, scouring rocky slopes to narrow washes and everything in between.

She looked up at the sky in an effort to concentrate on something besides her desire to see Ben Toomey. Father

Sky, Sadie had told her. Father Sky above her, Mother Earth at her feet. To walk in beauty—to be happy—she must always strive to be in harmony with them both and with every living thing there in and there on. Perhaps she was trying too hard. Ben had seemed to earnestly believe that she needed to be culturally acclimated. She, on the other hand, had no idea what she needed, except perhaps him.

She closed her eyes, trying to evoke some kinship with this homeland that supposedly she had been genetically programmed to want and need. She felt...nothing, except the warm sun on her face and the stirring of a breeze that brought with it the smell of dust and piñon pine.

When she opened her eyes, Sadie was watching her.

"The plants are like us," she said, continuing her lesson. "Like the People. They have their own clans and their own place to be. One grows good in the sunlight. One grows good in the rocks. If you ask with respect and listen for the answer, they will tell you which one you need to cure a sickness. You see?"

Eden didn't reply, because she had already learned that a response wasn't required. She was required only to listen and to learn.

"Maybe we should try to find out which clan *you* belong to," Sadie said.

"I don't think that's possible."

"It would be a good thing to know."

"Why?"

"So you can know who to marry, for one thing. Marrying in your own clan is taboo."

Eden smiled. "Right now I'm too busy trying to remember which is the bean plant and which is the owl's claw to worry about marrying."

"You never know. Marriages can sneak up on you."

"Did one sneak up on you?"

"Like a bolt of lightning from a blue sky," Sadie said.

"Didn't you want to get married?"

"Yes, I wanted to get married. And I wanted him. But I thought he wanted my cousin. She was beautiful. I was plain. It's scary for a plain woman to get the one she wants so bad."

"Was he a good husband?"

"Sometimes. He tried hard. Men don't know much about being husbands, you know. Some don't ever learn. But it's the trying that counts. A woman can overlook a lot—if he's trying. What is this?" Sadie asked abruptly, pointing to a fuzzy-leafed plant.

"That is...hunter's tobacco."

"And what would I use hunter's tobacco for?"

"To take away the human smell—so the prey doesn't know you're coming. Sort of like Chanel No 5—in reverse."

Eden glanced at Sadie to see if she was right. The old woman was smiling.

"You learn this good," she said. "Fast. Another fifteen years—who knows? Maybe you know more than me."

"I like knowing," Eden said.

Sadie made a soft sound that Eden had come to equate with "I understand" or "oh, really?" or "is that so?"

"I'm wondering," Sadie said. "Why do you work in a bank if you like to know about plants?"

"Investment counseling is where the money is."

"You need a lot of money, Eden Trevoy?"

"I used to think so," she said. "Now I'm not so sure."

The truth of the matter was that she wasn't sure about anything anymore—except that she wanted to see Ben.

"How do you do this thing—this investment counseling?"

"Well, people come into the bank with their money—and I tell them which companies would be good to invest in. If the company stays good, then they get more money back than they spent."

"And that makes them happy?"

"Very happy," Eden said.

Sadie made the soft sound again. "I think that's enough," she said, sticking one final root into her leather pouch. "We can go back now. You drive. I think we need a little excitement."

"Sadie, I can't drive that truck."

"I know. That's where the excitement comes in."

"I can't drive that truck," she said again.

"You can learn."

"What if I break something?"

"So what? You got money you don't know if you need or not. You can fix it."

Eden couldn't argue with logic like that, and once she got through the initial scraping of gears, she rather enjoyed the effort. She had always driven fast, and when she pulled onto a flat, straight stretch of paved road, she didn't make an exception of Sadie's well-used truck. They hurtled along, full-out, windows down, hair blowing in the wind.

And they both heard the siren at the same time, a white Navajo Tribal Police vehicle rapidly gaining on them in the rearview mirror.

"We're going to have some excitement now," Sadie observed.

Eden gave her a look and began to slow down. "You don't suppose he's after somebody else?"

"You see somebody else?" Sadie asked pointedly.

No. Eden didn't. She hadn't even seen him. She pulled carefully off the road and onto the shoulder.

Sadie turned around to look as the police vehicle pulled in behind them.

"Is it anyone you know?" Eden asked, carefully skirting what she really wanted to ask.

Is it Ben?

"No," Sadie said. "I don't think I know this one at all."

The officer got out and walked to the truck. He bent down to look into the window. He was wearing sunglasses; Eden couldn't see his eyes.

"Yah-ta-hey," he said, more to Sadie than to her, then he continued in Navajo—questions, it seemed to Eden, all of which Sadie apparently answered. Then, he walked back and looked under the tarp in the truck bed. On both sides.

"I thought you didn't know him," Eden whispered.

"I don't. He's a very polite boy. He was telling me his born-for and born-to clans—which clan his mother and his father come from," she added, apparently to satisfy Eden's puzzled look. "And I told him the same thing. I told you. Clans are important to know."

"Should we say Ben is your grandson?"

"Not unless you want a lecture about driving too fast from *two* mad policemen," Sadie said.

"What is he looking for?"

"He thinks he has to check in case we might be hauling water."

"Why would he care if we haul water?"

"Whiskey," Sadie said. "He thinks we're bootleggers."

"Bootleggers!" A speeding ticket was one thing. Being arrested for trafficking a controlled substance was something else again. "We're not, are we? Hauling water?"

"Not today," Sadie said mildly, and it wasn't until she suddenly grinned that Eden realized she was being shamelessly teased. They were both still laughing when the officer came back to the window. He briefly lifted his sunglasses, and Eden realized immediately that *she* was the one who knew him. His name escaped her, and she didn't try to see his name tag—but he had been at Ben's trailer with Angelina and Faye that afternoon.

"I need to see your driver's license, miss," he said, giving no indication that he recognized her.

Eden found it and gave it to him. He looked at her and at the picture. Several times.

"Do you know how fast you were going, Ms. Trevoy?" he asked in English.

"Too fast," Eden confessed. "I'm very sorry."

"I said I wanted excitement," Sadie put in. "She gave me some."

He gave them both a look. After a moment he handed back the license.

"Maybe you two ladies should try bingo," he said. "In the future be a little more careful on the highway, okay?"

Eden sat there, unable to believe her good fortune. After a moment she started the truck and jerkily drove away. She kept glancing at Sadie as she drove—well within the speed limit this time, because the police vehicle was trailing behind.

"What's the matter?" Eden finally asked her.

"Bingo," Sadie said. "Bingo is for *old* people."

They spent the rest of the afternoon sorting and processing all the plants and roots Sadie had collected, an opportunity for review, Eden realized, and to learn about the next step on the long road to becoming an accomplished Navajo herbalist. She was having no difficulty identifying the plants; accepting the concept of talking to them was something else again. That was the part that would likely take her fifteen years.

At one point the dogs rushed out toward the corral in a frenzy of barking. Sadie immediately reached for her long walking stick, expecting to have to contend with some predator about to lay claim to the sheep.

But it was someone on horseback, someone the dogs soon recognized and began to welcome as enthusiastically as they had just tried to scare him away.

Ben.

He was riding bareback, and he took his time approaching, maneuvering the horse along in the direction he wanted with seemingly little effort. He pulled just short of the place where Sadie sat, and he paid no attention to Eden at all. He spoke only to his grandmother, and he spoke in Navajo, so that Eden had no idea what passed between them. She could only tell that, in this conversation, Sadie Benally had suddenly become very much the head of the family.

There was a long and heavy silence, and Eden suspected that whatever had transpired, neither of them had gotten what they wanted. Then, Ben nudged the horse forward again, until it stopped much too close to her for her comfort. She had no idea what he thought he was doing. She didn't move, however.

Just when she had had enough and was about to say so, he extended his hand. She looked at it and then at him.

"You need a break," he said.

She surprised herself—and perhaps him—by reaching up without hesitation, letting him grip her arm firmly and swing her around behind him. The horse pranced under her added weight, and it took her a moment to get her seat. She didn't quite know where to put her hands and finally opted for hanging on to the back of his belt.

He brought the horse around, and without a word to his

grandmother, they headed back in the direction he had come at the same leisurely pace.

She assumed that he had something he wanted to tell her. They were far enough away from the compound now, but he didn't say a word. Nothing.

"Where are we going?" she asked finally.

"I thought you'd never ask," he said—but he still didn't tell her.

Okay, fine, she thought—because the truth of the matter was that she didn't care. She relaxed her death grip on his belt, letting her body sag into the rhythm of the horse's gait. And, in spite of everything she could—should—do, she leaned closer.

He smelled of soap and clean clothes that had been dried in the sun and wind. She was completely unprepared for the intensity of her response. She was nearly overcome by a sudden wave of sadness, and yet she was so glad to see him. She wanted to wrap her arms around him and press her face against his back.

What would he do if she did that? she wondered. What would he do if she wrapped her arms around him and cried all over his white T-shirt?

She indulged herself by looking at him instead. The back of his head and the haircut he had suffered for his sister's sake. His neck. Sometimes the side of his face when he looked to the left or right. He had long eyelashes, something she hadn't noticed before. And she could see just how long from this vantage point.

She realized that he was taking her on that same path through the red rock monoliths. It should have been easier in this direction, because they were on horseback and because it was mostly downhill. But the sharp downward slope meant that she slid firmly against him. She struggled briefly, but her legs were pressed into his, whether she wanted them to or not.

He seemed not to notice.

"You're learning," he said as the horse picked its way along.

"Learning?" she asked, thinking he meant something about the way she was sitting the horse.

He glanced at her over his shoulder. "To be Navajo."

"What makes you say that?"

"We've come all this way and you've only asked one question."

"Which you didn't answer," she said. "I might ask more—if I thought it would do any good."

"See?" he said, as if she'd just proved his point.

"No," she assured him.

"Well, there was a time when you wouldn't have recognized the futility of it," he said. "Today, you not only recognized it, you accepted it."

"You're full of you-know-what, Toomey," she said, and he laughed.

"Still protecting my virgin ears, I see."

She waited until they had ridden a little farther. "You said I couldn't ever be Navajo."

"Did I?"

"You know you did."

"Then I meant it—at the time. I didn't think you would try so hard."

She was both pleased and offended by the remark. "I told you my taking you up on your offer wasn't a whim."

"Yes, but there are whims and whims."

"What is that supposed to mean?"

"It means that a rich white girl might not know what a whim is."

"Are you deliberately trying to insult me?"

"No, I'm trying to take you to dinner."

"Dinner," she repeated, not sure she'd heard right.

"That's what I said."

"Where?"

He glanced at her over his shoulder again. "Well, it won't be Étienne's."

Actually, it was Chez Benjamin. He had bought a very large take-out pizza and a bottle of wine. Her contribution to the evening was to put the horse into the corral while he did the last-minute preparations.

"I·didn't want to get too cocky," he said. "It's kind of embarrassing to eat by yourself at a table set for two."

It pleased her that he had been uncertain about whether or not she'd come, just as it displeased her that he obviously needn't have worried. He hadn't given her much indication of what he had in mind, but clearly it hadn't mattered. She had been only too eager to jump on the back of a horse with him. And it annoyed her to no end that he had referred to her as a "rich white girl." She was only half white apparently.

Half.

She sighed heavily. She couldn't discount the way she had been raised—white to the point of snobbery, and she *was* rich, even without her job at the bank and the portion of Edna's trust fund that had been set aside for college scholarships. For all intents and purposes, Eden couldn't deny that she was exactly what Ben Toomey said she was—a rich white girl. And that was something she would never thank Edna for. If Edna had told the truth, and if Eden had been allowed to grow up out here, to learn first-hand about her father's people, even if it had to be without him, everything wouldn't be so difficult now.

And she wouldn't have had any reason to be worried about her increasing interest in Ben Toomey, an interest that admittedly began before she had any idea of her own heritage.

I don't understand, she kept thinking. I don't even like him. He's—

Exactly what was he? she wondered. Kind? Decent? More or less immune to her heretofore unfailing young charms? Oh, he *looked* at her when he thought she wouldn't notice. She had caught him at it enough to know that he wasn't entirely indifferent to her. She thought that he might actually like what he saw. It was just that he seemed…*immune*. Like a man already taken.

Angelina, she supposed—whose cleavage could launch a thousand ships. Eden looked down at her own chest and sighed. Comparatively speaking, she couldn't launch a dinghy.

When she returned to the trailer, he did indeed have the table set, and the background music consisted entirely of the radio she'd heard through the window the last time she was here, the one monitoring all the tribal police traffic in the area. The eating space was small, but the table had been placed in front of a large window with a magnificent view of the buttes and the huge thunderhead of an approaching storm. She tried to help with the meal, but she was in the way more often than not.

"None for me," he said when she would have poured him a glass of the wine. "I don't drink."

"Never?"

"Never."

"Why not?"

He looked at her a moment before he answered. "Because I don't want to end up lying in a park someplace and getting my brains kicked out by a bunch of white boys with nothing better to do."

For once in her life, she was at a loss for words.

What is this? she thought.

His remarks about the rich white girl and Étienne's pushed the edge of politeness. But this one was calculated and deliberately provocative.

He turned abruptly away from her to get the pizza box from the insulated bag he must have talked somebody into letting him keep. The pizza was still warm and it smelled wonderful.

"I didn't get anything too fancy," he said. "Just the basics. You do like pizza?"

She looked at him, trying to decide if this was another barb. No, she decided, and she tried to smile, tried to think that he wasn't being deliberately insulting.

"I have only one question," she said.

"What's that?"

"Where's yours?"

They were both hungry, and the conversation lagged while they ate. Thunder rumbled in the distance from time to time.

"This was a really good idea," she said at one point.

"I remembered when I was away at the university. I was always homesick for something familiar to eat."

She looked at him. Their eyes met, only this time he didn't look away as she would have expected. It was she who grew uncomfortable.

"Nice view," she said, looking out the window.

"You think so," he said. It wasn't quite a question, and it was a sarcastic response if she had ever heard one.

His eyes were waiting when she looked back.

"And you've got a nice place here," she said, still trying. Her gaze shifted away to look around the trailer.

"Yeah," he said, smiling slightly.

"It is," she insisted. "I like it."

"Why?"

"Why?"

"That's what I said. Why?"

It was obvious that he didn't believe for a minute that she had a reason, other than some token attempt to show off her boarding-school manners, for saying what she said.

"Because it's very retro. Very fifties. Or maybe sixties. And somebody has put a lot of work into it."

"Fifties," he said. He told her about the old man and woman and how he happened to buy it.

"How sad," she said.

"Depends on how you look at it. Their time together here was over, yes. But you have to think about all the years they had."

"Is that the Navajo mind-set again?"

"No, that's the Ben Toomey mind-set."

"Which mind-set bought the pizza?"

He smiled and didn't answer.

"So do you like doing...whatever it is you do?" he asked. "For a living, I mean."

"Investment banking. I don't know if I like it or not. I'm good at it—and it was as far away from archaeology as I could get. That seemed to be the most important thing—at the time. Do you like being a cop?"

"Yeah."

"Why?"

"Why?"

"That's what I said," she assured him. "Why? Or are you the only one who gets to ask that?"

"Okay. Because it matters. A lot more than wanting to annoy your mother or trying to divorce well."

"Touché," she said. "Again. You're determined to get your jabs in, aren't you?"

He flushed slightly. "I don't know what you mean."

"Oh, you know what I mean. This was a mistake, wasn't it?" She stood up and began to clear the table.

"Eden—" he said, standing as well and taking things out of her hands.

"Thank you for dinner," she said, and she made a point of avoiding his eyes. "It was quite a surprise—believe me—and in more ways than one."

"Wait," he said, when she headed for the door. "Wait!" He caught her by the arm. "I'm sorry if you thought—"

"If *I* thought? I'm not taking the blame for your rudeness, Toomey. I was insensitive that day after the memorial service—but at least I had some kind of excuse and I did apologize for it. I can't help what I am, and *I'm* sorry if you choose to be offended by it. I'm only here by invitation. You're the one who came looking for me, remember?" She pulled her arm free and sidestepped him to get to the door. She looked back at him before she went outside. "Like you said—have a nice life."

"Wait," he said again. "It's going to rain. I'll take you back to the compound in the truck."

She stared at him. "Thank you," she said evenly. "That would be...surprisingly kind."

She didn't hesitate. She stepped outside and walked rapidly to the truck. The door was locked, and she had to wait for him to get in and unlock it from the inside. It suddenly began to rain, an abrupt and heavy downpour. She was drenched by the time she got into the truck. She sat shivering against the door, as far away from him as possible.

The rain pounded the truck as he backed around. The radio was playing, but she could barely hear it. And she could barely see out the windshield. She glanced at him. He stared straight ahead, his face grim, his jaw tight.

There was no conversation on the way; it was a relief

when they reached his grandmother's place. She immediately moved to get out of the truck, raining or not.

"It was good old Navajo guilt," he said abruptly as she opened the door.

"What?"

"It was guilt—the reason I was being such a jerk."

"What have you got to feel guilty about?" she asked, expecting him to verify what she had suspected earlier— that he was "taken."

"Sadie doesn't approve of my being with you like this."

"Why?" she asked in surprise.

It took him a long time to answer.

"She thinks I want you," he said finally, his eyes looking directly into hers. She could feel her heart begin to pound, her belly grow warm. It was all she could do not to look away. She was afraid suddenly—not of him—of herself—but she still asked.

"Do you?"

The rain beat down harder. She barely heard him. Her hand rested on the seat between them. His fingertips just touched hers.

"Yeah," he said.

Chapter Eight

I shouldn't have said it, he thought yet another time. He sat at his desk and stared at the file cabinet. He *never* should have told Eden that he wanted her. Never. She had only looked at him, and then she went running out into the rain and into his grandmother's house—where he couldn't follow. He wouldn't have told her—maybe—if she hadn't been so upset with him, if she hadn't already been thinking the worst of him. She had wanted a reason, and he had given her one.

So much for thinking the worst.

Her low opinion of him *before* he made his little announcement would be nothing compared to her opinion of him now. And he couldn't explain anything to her; he couldn't even explain it to himself. The only thing he knew for certain was that he had told her the truth.

He wanted Eden Trevoy.

All the time. And these past few days, he had been a

pitiful and miserable human being because of it. She was the only thing on his mind. He wanted her in that pink-flowered dress, so he could have the exquisite pleasure of getting her out of it. He wanted to lie with her all night in his narrow bed. He wanted to make love with her. He wanted to be the best she ever had. He wanted to be the *last* she ever had.

What a joke, he thought. The orphaned heiress and the tribal cop. Only he didn't feel like laughing. Neither would his family, and neither, he suspected, would she.

"Toomey!" Lucas Singer yelled behind him.

"Sir!" he said, startled.

"We've got a call about a man with a gun—possible shots fired at cars passing on the road." Lucas handed him a slip of paper. "Here's the last reported location. Take Joey Nez with you."

"Yes, sir," Toomey said.

"And be careful. And don't do anything stupid. If you need more backup, you call in."

"Yes, sir," he said again.

Joey was already waiting for him in the parking lot, clearly excited by the prospect of something besides doling out speeding tickets.

"I'll drive," Joey said hopefully.

"You'll ride," Toomey answered.

"I'll ride," Joey decided.

"You ever been on anything like this before?" Joey asked as they drove away.

"Yeah," Toomey said.

"What happened?"

"Captain Becenti—and Lucas—took the gun away from the guy before he killed somebody."

"What were you doing?"

"I was supposed to take him out if things went bad and they couldn't do it."

"Oh," he said, some of his previous enthusiasm fading. "You think you could do that—shoot a man?"

"If I can't, I've got no business being here."

They rode for a time in silence.

"Ben?"

"What?" he said, thinking that the last thing he wanted to deal with was Joey Nez with a case of cold feet.

"Is Eden Trevoy your woman?"

Toomey nearly ran off the road. "Where the hell did that come from?"

"I stopped her for speeding a couple of days ago. Your grandmother was with her. And she came out to your place the other day, so I thought maybe—"

"Well, you thought wrong."

"She's not then?"

"No," Toomey said grimly. "She's not."

"Good. Great. I guess you won't care if I ask her out then."

Toomey looked at him. Clearly, Joey Nez didn't feel any of the constraints *he* did. Joey didn't care in the least about the vast difference in his and Eden Trevoy's backgrounds. Joey simply liked what he saw and he wanted more. Nothing complicated there. He would boldly ask Eden to go someplace with him without the least hesitation—he would probably take her line dancing, maybe he would even suggest a Nez-Toomey double date. Apparently, the only thing that had stood in his way was verbal permission from his friend and fellow officer, good old Ben Toomey.

"She's got a lot of class," Joey said.

"Yeah? What do you know about class?"

"I mean it. She didn't even try to talk me out of giving

her a ticket—and she's bound to know she's good looking enough to do it, don't you think?''

Toomey didn't answer.

"So what do you think I ought to do?''

"About what?''

"About Eden Trevoy! What do you think we're talking about here?''

Toomey wasn't talking about anything. He was only trying to do what he was supposed to do—find the man with the gun and the inclination to use it—and not smack Joey Nez upside the head in the process.

"How hot do you think she is?'' Joey persisted.

"Listen, Joey. She's not my woman—yet. Understand?''

"Unit four-seven-three, Chinle,'' the radio broke in before Joey could say whether he did or didn't.

"Four-seven-three. Go ahead, Chinle,'' Toomey said, grateful for the interruption.

"Please be—location—''

He gave their approximate location, taking a guess at what the dispatcher wanted and hoping the transmission from Chinle wouldn't get any worse.

"Chinle units have the—blocked—five miles ahead of you. Please be advised—second roadblock—at your present location.''

Toomey verified what he thought Chinle wanted.

"Okay,'' he said to Joey. "Looks like we're open for business.''

"You think the shooter is between us and the Chinle guys?''

"I guess so,'' Toomey said as he made a U-turn and parked across the highway. "Sounds like they've got a location on him. Anyway, they don't want civilians driving into the middle of this.''

"Ben?" the radio cracked when he was about to get out.

He immediately recognized the voice and reached for the hand mike. "Yeah, Mary, what?"

"Faye was in here—ago—"

"Say again?" he said. "Faye what?"

"—haircut—talk to—mother and grandmother—really upset—"

He stared at the hand mike for a moment, as if it would help. "I didn't get that, Mary. What about a haircut?"

"Faye gave—haircut—she needs—talk to—mother and grandmother—"

"She gave my mother and grandmother a haircut?"

"No!"

"Mary, your transmission is breaking up—"

"—got an A."

"What the hell does that mean?" he said to himself.

"Mary," he said, keying the mike, "you're going to have to give me this again when I'm in a better location—"

"Vehicle coming, Ben," Joey said.

"I've got a customer, Mary. Four-seven-three, clear," he said. He was certainly intrigued, but he would have to worry about the latest haircut crisis later. He chuckled as he got out, wondering who the victim was this time.

"I'll talk to him," he said to Joey as the truck slowed. "You watch for anything coming in the other direction."

He motioned for the driver to stop and walked in that direction.

"Yah-ta-hey," he said as he approached.

The man didn't reply, and Toomey realized two things too late and at the same instant. The man was drunk, and the man had a shotgun across his lap.

He saw the barrel of the gun come up, and his mind presented him with a single crazy thought.

"Ben's Song"—I think it's a funeral dirge.

"Let me see," Mary Skeets said.

Eden stepped closer and turned her head to give Mary a better view.

"Well, it's cute as can be," Mary said, "but I can see why Sadie was so upset."

"Then tell me," Eden said. At Sadie's insistence, she had come to the law enforcement building looking for Faye—who had come to the law enforcement looking for Ben.

"She's very traditional," Mary said. "One of the old beliefs is that a woman's wisdom is in her hair."

Eden reached up to run her fingers through her freshly shorn locks. "In that case, I must be dumb as dirt, huh?"

"That's about the size of it. Sadie sees it as a very bad thing for Faye to do to you."

"But I was just trying to help her with one of her exams. I didn't know it would cause all this uproar."

"Well, Faye did. She knew good and well her mother and Sadie would have a fit if she cut your hair off. That girl is a handful—and she always expects Benjamin to get her out of it. I think she's going to make a decent beautician, though. That style is really cute on you—it's a lot better cut than the one she gave Benjamin, let me tell you. You look so different. I almost didn't know you."

Eden took a deep breath and tried to sound nonchalant. "Do you know if Faye talked to Ben?"

"No, he was out on a call. He still is. He should have radioed in by now. I'm getting a little worried—"

The telephone rang, and she answered it.

She listened for a moment, then abruptly stood up and

leaned over the counter. "Lucas!" she yelled at the top of her voice.

Lucas Singer immediately stepped out of his office. "For God's sake, Mary! The building does have a phone system—"

"Two officers down!" Mary yelled.

"Who?" Lucas said, coming rapidly in their direction.

"I don't know. This is Hosteen Nakai—he won't talk to me—he wants you," she said, handing him the telephone. "It must be Benjamin and Joey."

"Ben?" Eden said, trying to get Mary's attention. "Mary, did you say it was Ben?"

Mary held up her hand. They both stared at Lucas while he talked on the telephone. The conversation was in Navajo.

"What is he saying?" Eden asked, but Mary ignored her.

Lucas hung up the phone. "Get my wife," he said to Mary. "Tell her they're bringing one of them to the clinic."

"Who?" Eden said, stepping up to him.

He looked at her blankly, then abruptly frowned when he recognized her and waved her away.

"If it's Ben Toomey, you tell me!" she cried, refusing to step aside.

"I don't know who it is, Ms. Trevoy. And I don't have time for this." He moved around her and walked hurriedly back toward his office. "Mary, make sure you notify Captain Becenti!" he called before he disappeared inside.

"Right!"

Eden stood there, not knowing what to do. She could only wait until Mary had finished all her notifications.

"I want to go to the clinic. Where is it?" Eden said

when Mary finally looked at her. "Please," she added, because she could feel Mary's resistance.

After a moment Mary quickly scribbled the directions on a piece of paper and tore it off.

"Thank you," Eden said, looking down at it. She gave a heavy sigh.

"It may not be him," Mary said. "Hosteen Nakai— he's an old man. He doesn't read English. He couldn't read a name tag if they weren't able to tell him—" She abruptly stopped. "If you find out anything at the clinic, will you call me here?"

Eden nodded and hurried out the door. The clinic wasn't hard to find. She didn't want to hang around the parking lot; she went inside immediately. A few Navajo people sat in the waiting area, and a young girl with a clipboard—a volunteer from one of the high schools, Eden guessed— immediately approached.

"May I help you?" she asked.

"No, I—well, maybe. I'm a friend of Officer Ben Toomey's. I think he's been hurt and they may be bringing him here. I'd like to wait."

The girl looked startled. This scenario didn't fit anything she had on her clipboard. "I'll ask Mrs. Singer," she said.

The girl didn't return. An attractive woman in a white lab coat came instead, a woman who likely would show her the door. Eden hadn't had much rapport of late with people named Singer.

"Please," she began before the woman said anything. "Don't throw me out. I promise I'll stay out of the way. I won't be any trouble. I just need to know if he's okay."

"No, no. I'm not going to throw you out. You can wait in here—who did you say you were?"

"A friend of Ben Toomey's."

"No, I meant your name."

"Eden Trevoy."

"Oh, yes," the woman said. "I was very sorry to hear about your mother."

"You knew her?"

"I patched her up a few times when she got hurt out at the digs. She was an incredible woman—but she was the biggest klutz."

Eden smiled at the woman's very accurate assessment of Edna's gracelessness, and she forgot for a moment why she was here and what her relationship with Edna had been. But her amusement quickly faded.

"I was at the law enforcement building when the call came in. I'm not even sure it's Ben," she said.

"We'll just have to wait and see. Have you known him long?"

"No—not long. Well, we met when we were children. And then not again until recently."

"He's a good officer—according to my husband," the woman said. "Let's not worry until we have to."

"Lieutenant Singer is your husband," Eden said to verify what she now suspected. But what really surprised her was the fact that Mrs. Singer obviously wasn't Navajo. So much for her theory that Lucas Singer's animosity toward her was because he thought she was white.

"Yes. You've met him I take it," the woman said.

"Well, sort of. I think he'd rather I stayed out of the police station unless I'm the victim of a crime—is that them?" Eden said in alarm, because of the sudden commotion outside the front door. Several people were coming in, none of whom she recognized. She kept trying to see. Lucas Singer was holding open the door, and Ben—Ben was walking under his own power.

But he looked terrible. His arm was bleeding, and several places on his face. He was clearly dazed; Lucas Singer had to steer him in the right direction.

Mrs. Singer stepped forward, and Eden would have gone with her.

"Wait," Mrs. Singer said. "You were going to stay out of the way, remember? Don't worry. I'll tell him you're here."

Eden nodded, but it was all she could do not to go to him. She stood there, relieved but still afraid. When he was about to go through the double doors to the treatment area, he suddenly looked back over his shoulder.

"Eden!" he called.

She rushed forward in spite of her promise. "Ben, are you okay?" she asked, reaching out to touch him, but stopping short because she was afraid she might hurt him.

"Yeah—" he said. He tried to smile and didn't quite make it.

"Let's go, Toomey," Lucas Singer said to him. "This is not the time."

"No—wait," Ben said. "Eden, will you—do something for me?"

"Yes, of course. What?"

"Go tell my mother and Sadie—I'm—all right."

"Okay," she said.

"Here," he said, fumbling with some keys he had on his belt. He stepped toward her to give them to her. "Wait for me." He pressed the keys into her hand; his hand was shaking. "At—my place, okay? Wait—will you do that?"

"All right," she said.

"I don't know how long I'll—" He broke off and looked around, as if he were a little surprised to find himself here.

"I'll wait," she said.

"Good. Good. I'll see you—later." He managed a slight smile after all. "So—you're it."

"What?" she asked, not understanding.

"The haircut—"

But Lucas Singer urged him away. She stood there with the keys in her hand, and she didn't miss the look Lucas gave her as the double doors closed after them.

"She's not here," Lucas said. His tone of voice suggested that he was not in the least surprised.

Toomey didn't say anything. He could see perfectly well for himself that Eden's car wasn't anywhere around. He fought down his disappointment and opened the police vehicle door.

"I can take you back to your mother's place. You shouldn't be by yourself. You're not going to just sit here and wait for her, are you?"

Toomey ignored the question. "Thanks for the ride home, sir. If you hear anything about Joey, I'd appreciate it if you'd let me know. I don't care what time it is."

"This girl is not good for you, Toomey."

"Sir, with all due respect, there is no way in hell you could possibly know that."

"I've been down this road, and I'm telling you—"

"Lieutenant, you are way out of line here!"

"Maybe so. But I know what I'm talking about. The differences between the two of you are too strong. She won't be able to overcome them."

"Your wife is a white woman. She overcame the 'differences,' didn't she?"

"It's not the same thing. I wasn't traditional, and Sloan had ties here."

"So does Eden."

"Having a mother who spent her whole life trying to

resurrect the Old Ones isn't a tie. And I'm not talking about Sloan. I'm talking about...someone else. Sloan was never like this woman or Eden Trevoy.''

''You don't know what Eden is like. You don't know anything about her.''

''The Trevoy girl has had way too much money for her own good, Toomey. You're the latest toy. It's only a matter of time before she gets bored with you and everything you represent.''

''You don't know that.''

''I do know it. You think she understands anything about who and what you are? She'll be proud of herself for getting your attention, and then she's going to get bored, and she's going to move on.''

''I don't want to talk about this,'' Toomey said. He got out and closed the door. He was so tired suddenly.

''Toomey—''

''No,'' he said.

He walked to the front door without looking back, wondering how he was going to get in. He had given Eden his key.

''Ben!''

He looked around. Faye was approaching rapidly on her pinto mare. She reined in sharply and slid quickly off the horse's back.

''Ben, are you okay? Eden said you were, but—'' She stopped, her eyes going to his bloody uniform.

''Where is she?'' he said. ''Her car's not here.''

''You're not mad at me, are you? Because I cut her hair? She wanted me to. And she said it was okay, Ben. Really, she did. Mom and Grandma—well, you don't want to hear what *they* said. But I got an A, Benjy. An honest-to-God A!''

"Faye," he said with a patience he didn't begin to feel, "why isn't Eden here?"

"Well, that's kind of a long story—"

"For once—do you think you could just answer a simple question?"

"Which question, Benjy?"

He swore—in English, because the Navajo language had no appropriate words to express his degree of aggravation.

"She's watching the fire, Benjamin," Faye said.

"What fire!"

Her eyes went to his uniform again. "Grandma Sadie said you had to go into the sweat lodge as soon as you got here. She said you'd looked at death and you needed—"

He didn't stay to listen. He walked off toward the mud and timber sweat lodge he had built a short distance away from the trailer.

"Go home, Faye," he said over his shoulder.

"Home?"

"Please."

"Well, okay. I'll go. Is Eden coming with me?"

"No, Faye, she isn't," he said—without having the slightest idea whether he was telling the truth or not.

Thankfully, Faye apparently grasped the situation. "Oh," she said. "Do you want me to tell Mom and Grandma Sadie anything?"

He looked at her.

"Oh," she said again.

He gave her a final wave—the lieutenant, too, if he was still watching—and he kept walking. The sun was almost gone. He could see the glow of the fire in the shallow pit, smell the smoke from the burning wood. And finally, he could see Eden, sitting on a nearby stump, with a pitchfork over her knees. She stood immediately.

"I think it's ready," she said.

He didn't say anything.

She gave a small, apologetic shrug. "Sadie said if I was going to be here, I should do something useful."

He kept staring at her—and her little-boy haircut. She was beautiful to him, shorn or not. She looked so different and yet vaguely familiar. He tried and failed to remember if she had ever worn her hair cropped off like this when they were children.

And he realized suddenly that she was indeed learning. She was waiting now, for him to speak or stay silent, as he chose, and with an acceptance that belied the worry he saw in her eyes.

After a moment he began to unbutton his ruined uniform shirt. His right arm hurt like hell, and she dropped the pitchfork and stepped forward to help him. He could smell her soft woman scent. He wanted to touch her. It was all he could do not to touch her.

What was happening to him?

He hadn't thought once about needing the sweat lodge. He had only thought about how much he needed *her*. Knowing she was here, waiting, was the only thing that had gotten him through the ordeal of reliving what had happened out there on the road, the questions and more questions, and then telling it all again to Joey's mother.

Lucas Singer hadn't pointed out any dire consequences of a relationship with Eden Trevoy that he himself hadn't already anticipated. He knew that he couldn't have her for long—if at all. He understood that either way it would only be a matter of time before she went back to her real life. The truth of the matter was that she would be there now if he hadn't intervened.

But he still wanted her, no matter how long it lasted. And he knew in his heart that right now was the beginning of whatever lay before them.

She took the shirt away, then helped him with his undershirt.

"What about Joey?" she asked, and he shook his head.

"I don't think he'll..." He stopped and took a ragged breath, torn between not wanting to talk about it anymore and wanting to tell her everything.

"Damned fool didn't do what he was supposed to do," he said finally, letting the thing he hadn't told anyone tumble out. "He should have gotten out of there, but he...came running to help me. Lucas said they caught the guy. He was passed out in his truck—just a little way down the road. And the son of a bitch isn't even going to remember what he—"

He stopped, the memory of Joey's wounding akin to physical pain. He abruptly lifted back the blankets that covered the entrance to the sweat lodge. He did need this. He had to hold on to something.

He moved away from her and picked up the pitchfork, and he began to rake the stones out of the fire and carry them into the lodge. This time she made no attempt to help. When that was done, he put the pitchfork aside, and he reached out to turn her in the opposite direction, so that she was facing the monoliths.

"Your virgin eyes," he said, careful not to touch her any longer than was necessary.

Then, he left her standing, and he unbuckled his belt and took off his boots and pants, stripping naked. The night air was cold on his skin, and he shivered. The chant—the *Hozhonji* song—the "Mountain Song"—was already in his mind. It was the first song he had ever learned, passed down through generation after generation of the People and taught to him by his father in keeping with the Old Ways.

Thither go I!

Chief of all mountains,
Thither go I!

But there would be no purification, no blessing if he lost his concentration and made a mistake. He forced himself to let go of everything but the song. All his disharmony. All the anger he felt at Lucas Singer's interference. All the horror of this day and the look on Joey Nez's face.

And the desire for the woman who would only cause him pain.

The moon was up when he finally staggered out of the sweat lodge. The ritual had left him exhausted. He didn't see Eden anywhere, and he had no idea how much time had passed. He reached down to pick up his clothes and a blanket she must have left for him. He felt dazed and weak, and he stood there in the cold night air, gathering his strength, gathering the courage to go and see if he was as alone as he felt.

There were no lights on in the trailer, and he forced himself to walk in that direction. He didn't call out to her, not then and not when he went inside. He stood for a moment by the door, listening, but he couldn't hear her, couldn't feel her presence.

He went directly into the shower to complete the purification ritual, remembering just in time that he had a bandaged arm.

He felt better when he stepped out—at least until he verified once and for all that Eden had gone. He put on cutoff jeans and wandered around inside the trailer and out, looking for her, for a note, for *something* and shamelessly listening for the sound of an approaching car.

He supposed that she must have walked back to the family compound, or perhaps his mother and Sadie, ever mindful of proper Navajo decorum, had come and taken her away. What he didn't—wouldn't—suppose was that

Lucas Singer had been right. Toomey was far from ready to conclude that Eden had already lost interest in her newest "toy"—now that it had been noticeably dented if not actually broken—and she had moved on.

But Lucas would be happy to know that Toomey wouldn't just sit and wait for her. He was far too tired to do either one. He went back inside the trailer and lay down on his narrow bed, his good arm thrown over his eyes. He couldn't find a comfortable place to put his bandaged arm, because it throbbed and burned so, regardless of the position. He was certain that there were things he should do, but he couldn't call to mind any of them. He had the pills Lucas's wife had given him to take for the pain, but he didn't do that, either.

What was Joey doing right now? he wondered. Still trying not to die? Or already gone on that long journey to nowhere? Tomorrow he would go Albuquerque to the medical center at UNM to see him.

Where had she gone, damn it! Back to Albuquerque? Maybe she'd had enough of being Navajo. Maybe she—

Eden!

"What?" she said, and he abruptly opened his eyes. The lamp was still on; he could see her plainly.

"You called my name," she said. "Are you all right?"

He stared at her. Had he been asleep? He must have been. He certainly hadn't realized that she had returned or that he had spoken aloud.

She stood there, waiting for him to explain.

"I—" he began, but he couldn't do it. How could he explain the unexplainable to her or to himself? He drew a wavering breath. "It's...nothing."

"Did you want something? Are you in pain?"

"No," he said.

"You're not telling me the truth."

He sighed. His eyes held hers; he didn't look away. "Where did you go?" he asked to change the subject.

"Faye brought my car—I ran out of gas just a little way from your grandmother's place. And then I took her and your brother Paul back to the compound."

"My brother Paul was here?"

"For a little while. He said he couldn't interrupt you while you were in the sweat lodge and he had to get back to Flagstaff. He…just wanted to make sure you were all right."

"What did you tell him?"

"I told him you had one arm bandaged and you were walking around and talking—but you weren't all right."

"You shouldn't have said that."

"Why not? It's the truth. I know you well enough to see it."

"You don't know me at all. If you did, you'd—"

"I'd what?" she asked when he didn't go on.

"You'd get the hell out of here," he answered.

"Why? Are you planning on being a jerk again and hurting my feelings?"

"Eden—"

"You keep forgetting this same small detail, Toomey." He looked at her. "What?"

"I'm here by invitation."

"Don't you understand?" he said. "I want you to come to bed with me."

If his revelation surprised her, it didn't show. "I believe you mentioned that the other night," she said.

"And you ran off like a scared rabbit."

"Well, I'm not running now."

She placed one knee on the edge of the bed and then the other, crawling slowly forward until she could stretch out beside him.

"Don't start this, Eden," he warned her. "Not if you don't mean it." But even as he said it, he was gathering her to him with his good arm. Her arms went around him and he pressed his face into her neck, losing himself in her warmth and her soft woman smell, in the feel of her body against his.

Then, gently—ever so gently—he kissed her temple, and then both her eyes and the corner of her mouth. She drew a shaky breath and her lips parted.

"Too late now," he said.

His mouth found hers. The kiss was deep and urgent, hungry and a long time in coming.

She tasted so good to him!

He immediately began to tremble, his need for her rising much too fast. He had known that it would be like this the first time, that his desire for her would drive him hard to take everything and give nothing in return.

His hand slid upward to caress her breast. Through the thin material of her shirt he felt the nipple immediately harden. He lingered there until she gave a soft moan, and he marveled that she would let him kiss her and touch her like this, that she would return his kiss and his awkward, one-armed embrace.

It took a great deal of effort for him to lean back and look at her. "This is where you run away again," he said. "If you don't want—"

"What I want is you," she interrupted.

His eyes searched hers to see if she meant it. She reached to turn off the lamp.

"No, leave it on."

She pressed a kiss into the palm of his hand. "If I do, then it won't be the way I imagined."

He would have turned the light off himself, if he'd been able.

He kissed her again, his fingers fumbling at the buttons of her shirt. She abruptly sat up and took it off herself. Her bra was a kind of T-shirt material with an elastic band and no fasteners. She pulled it over her head. His breath caught at the sight of her. She had beautiful breasts. Perfect. His hands ached to touch them, but she twisted away from him and snapped off the light. He did his best to help her take off the rest of her clothes, struggled harder to get rid of his own. Then she reached for him in the darkness, sliding against him. Her warm breasts. Her smooth thighs. Her soft, soft belly.

"Tell me," he whispered urgently, his mouth tasting and tasting hers. "Tell me what you—imagined."

"Being in the dark—with you—here," she said, straining against him. "Feeling your hands—all over me—"

"How—about—'hand,'" he said, and she laughed softly in the darkness.

Then she reached up to gently stroke his face, her fingers moving lightly over his mouth. "I was so afraid for you," she said. "Oh, Ben—"

His arms tightened around her, and she clung to him. His bandaged arm was killing him. He didn't care. He could feel his control slipping away. He had survived, and therefore he had no time to waste.

They were both deadly serious now, frantic, trembling in their need for each other. Kissing and touching became incidental and far from enough. Her body was open and eager, rising under his caress.

He entered her quickly, the sensation sharp and sweet and more intense than anything in his not so vast experience. He moaned in pleasure, tried to give her time to adjust to him. He forgot the pain in his arm. He forgot everything but having her. He began to thrust into her, his desire primal and unrestrained. He tried to stay silent and couldn't. It was so good. *She* was so good—

She wrapped herself around him, arms and legs, and he plunged deeper into her. He was no longer aware of anything but the intense pleasure. He couldn't stop, couldn't hold back. In the last moment, he thought she cried out his name.

Chapter Nine

Eden awoke at first light, and she lay there, alert and listening. Ben was sleeping heavily beside her, his body curved around hers, his breath warm against her neck. She could hear the sound of footsteps outside. Someone Navajo, she thought, because there was no immediate pounding on the door. She slid carefully out from under Ben's arm, trying not to hurt him or wake him. He stirred slightly, and she pressed a soft kiss at the corner of his mouth before she got out of bed.

It was a mistake, of course, letting their so-called relationship progress to this point. Looking at him now, in the cold light of day, she knew that she should be filled with regret, but she wasn't. She had never felt about any man the way she felt about Ben Toomey, and yet she knew there was absolutely no future for them. Thanks to Edna, she had learned to be the consummate realist at a very early age. She knew perfectly well that a series of torrid one-night stands was the best that she and Ben could hope for, just as she knew she would remember their first night together for the rest of her life.

She could hear the person outside walking back and forth, and she searched for her clothes and quickly dressed. She was cold, and she picked up one of Ben's sweatshirts from a basket of clean laundry in the hallway and put it on. It was too big for her and hung nearly to her knees.

She opened the trailer door and stepped outside, just as the visitor was about to disregard proper decorum and knock.

Lucas Singer. The absolute last person she wanted to see this morning. It was obvious to her that he wasn't surprised to find her here. It was equally obvious that he disapproved.

"I need to talk to Toomey," he said without prelude.

"He's still asleep," she said. And she wasn't being deliberately contrary—yet. She was simply stating the truth. "I'll give him the message, if you want."

"What I want is to talk to him," Lucas said. "Now."

She took a deep breath. "Lieutenant Singer, would you kindly tell me exactly what it is you think I've done—"

"No," he said. He looked at her directly and without apology.

"I don't deserve this—"

"Neither does he," Lucas said.

"What is that supposed to mean?"

He didn't answer the question.

"I care about Ben," she said.

"Today, maybe. Maybe even tomorrow. What about next week, Ms. Trevoy? Next year? You haven't given it that much thought, have you? You have no idea of the pain you can cause him—and neither does he. Ben Toomey is hogan raised. His family is traditional. They follow the Old Ways. He was very carefully taught, so that he could walk in beauty always. But believe me, as carefully taught as he was, he didn't learn anything about surviving somebody like you.''

"You know, this is really none of your business—"

"Anything that interferes with his job is my business."

"I haven't interfered."

"No? You think if he'd had his mind on what he was supposed to be doing, he would have walked right into the business end of a shotgun? He's a better officer than that. Or he was."

"I am not the reason he was shot."

"No? His job performance is way off since he got tangled up with you."

"I don't believe you—"

They both looked around as the trailer door opened and Ben stepped outside.

"Lieutenant?" he said, looking from one of them to the other.

It was very clear to Eden that he knew that some kind of exchange had just occurred between her and Lucas Singer.

"Captain Becenti wants to see you," Lucas said.

"Now?" Ben asked.

"Toomey, have you ever known Becenti to want something any other way?"

"No, sir. I guess not. Have you...heard anything about Joey?"

"No. Nothing. I'll wait in the vehicle," Lucas said. "If you've got a clean uniform, I suggest you wear it."

He walked away, and Eden stared after him. She would have preferred to continue the discussion. Surely Lucas Singer didn't actually mean that she was partially responsible for Ben's being hurt.

No, she thought. Lucas Singer had meant that she was entirely responsible. She didn't want to even consider that it might be true.

She realized suddenly that Ben had said her name.

"What?"

"I asked if you're okay."

"I'm not the one who was shot, Toomey," she said without looking at him.

"Did Lucas say something to you?"

His tone of voice made her turn to him and force a smile. He had had troubles enough of late without her making him think he had to confront his lieutenant on her behalf.

"Yes. He said, 'I need to talk to Toomey,'" she answered, wondering as she said it if omission was indeed a lie.

"Is that all?"

"No. He said, 'Now.'" She ground out the *now,* making him smile. And she didn't miss the expression of profound relief that accompanied it.

"Please," she said, holding open the trailer door. "Do *not* keep that man waiting. Something tells me he doesn't like waiting any more than Captain...whoever."

"Becenti," Ben said. "Are you sure you're okay?"

She gave him a mischievous look and pulled the door closed behind them. "Why don't you say what you really mean, Officer?" she said, stepping close to him so he could enfold her with his uninjured arm.

"What do I really mean?" he asked, smiling down at her.

He was more himself this morning, and she was thankful for that, but he wasn't the imperturbable Ben Toomey she had met that night in the arroyo.

"You want to know if you're any good in the sack,"

she said, expecting her rich-girl audacity to catch him completely off guard.

It did.

"No," he said, as soon as he recovered. "Wrong. Absolutely not. But since you brought it up—"

They stood there, embracing, smiling into each other's eyes. He reached to stroke her face.

"Eden…"

Oh, God, she thought. If anything had happened to him—if she really had been the cause—

She leaned into him, offering him her mouth and anything else he wanted. His kiss was as hungry and arousing as if last night had never happened. The sudden onset of desire took her breath away.

But he was the one who stopped. He held her tightly, his breathing ragged.

"Lucas is—out there," he said, his mouth finding hers again.

"I know," she murmured.

"No, he's out there—" he insisted.

"I know," she said again.

"Then help me!" he said, and they both laughed, heads together like naughty children.

He took a deep breath and attempted to move away from her. "No more kissing."

"None?" she asked, pressing her body against his.

"You're the one who said I can't keep Lucas waiting—"

"Did I?"

He groaned, but he held on to his restraint.

"Why don't you go sit down over there?"

"I'd rather tag along with you," she teased.

"Eden—I can't—"

But he did, his mouth on hers one more time. Then he

placed his hand on her shoulder and turned her around facing the opposite direction. "Go that way. Please."

"Men are so fickle," she said, looking over her shoulder.

"That way," he said again, pointing her toward the couch in the living area.

"Are you sure?"

"No, I'm not sure! This is—it's too—if you don't—"

"Me, too," she said, smiling back at him. "All of that—and more."

She waited until she heard the shower running, and then she went back outside. Lucas Singer wasn't in the "vehicle" after all. He had gone down to the sweat lodge and he was standing near the fire pit, looking toward the red rock monoliths.

Eden walked in that direction, stopping nearby, but making no effort to speak to him. He didn't acknowledge her presence, and they both stood in silence.

"Where did you learn *that?*" he asked after a time, and she understood exactly what he meant. He hadn't expected her to know basic Navajo politeness, much less practice it.

"Sadie Benally is teaching me," she said.

"Why?"

"She thinks I need to know."

"She approves of you and Toomey, then?"

"You know better than that, Lieutenant," Eden said, recognizing that he had deliberately given her a golden opportunity to lie, to put him in the wrong by pretending that the very relationship he protested so vigorously was perfectly fine with Ben's family.

"Yes, I do. I know you aren't the kind of woman he was brought up to have anything to do with. And I know how hard it was for his family to let him go away to college. They made a lot of sacrifices for him because they thought he could help the People. Do you know anything about the People, Ms. Trevoy?"

She didn't respond to his thinly disguised sarcasm. "I told you," she said. "Sadie Benally is teaching me."

"Then she must not know what you really want."

"Tell me, Lieutenant. What do I really want?"

"You want to be amused, Ms. Trevoy."

"You're an authority on my inner motivation, I take it."

"Unfortunately, yes. Yours and women like you."

"Women like me?"

"Do you think Toomey will go against Sadie and his family for you?" he asked. "He'll have to, you know."

"I wouldn't ask him to."

"Ah," he said. "Very convenient. What if you don't have to ask him? What if he doesn't understand that you don't really mean anything you say, and he does it, anyway? Then what will you do?"

She had to walk away a few steps to keep her control.

"You said it was my fault—that he and Joey were shot—that he wasn't paying attention," she said after a moment. "Is Ben in trouble? Is that why you came to get him?"

It took him a long time to decide whether or not he wanted to answer her. "Becenti isn't satisfied with the report," he said finally.

"What could happen to him—to Ben—if Becenti thinks he was careless?"

"If he can't do his job, he won't be a tribal cop anymore," Lucas said bluntly.

Eden looked at him in alarm.

"No, that can't happen," she said. "You don't understand. The situation between Ben and me is not what you think."

He actually laughed.

"Ms. Trevoy," he said, still amused. "It is *exactly* what I think." He walked away a few steps, then turned back to her. "The person who doesn't understand is you. I would suggest that you talk to Toomey's grandmother. She can explain all these fine points you don't seem to grasp."

Eden stood there, watching him walk away, not knowing what to do. She still didn't understand Lucas Singer's animosity. So what if she and Ben were from different worlds. So were a lot of people. So apparently were Lucas Singer and his wife.

Ben came out of the trailer, and she hurried in his direction, knowing that Lucas was watching.

Am I? she thought. Am I that bad for Ben?

"Will you be here when I get back?" he asked as she fell into step with him.

"I'm not sure," she said, avoiding his eyes.

"If you're not, I'll come by Sadie's—"

"No, I think I really have to go."

Ben stopped walking. "Go where?"

She looked up at him. "Back to Albuquerque."

"I thought you had vacation time."

"I've used it—or most of it. I need to go. I have to be back at work and there are some things I have to do."

He was staring at her. She gave a small shrug.

"Well, when are you coming back?"

"I'm...not sure. I tell you what. Why don't you call me? I'm in the book." She smiled a smile she didn't begin to feel.

"Yeah," he said. "I can always do that. I can call you. No problem. Plenty of phones on the rez."

"Ben, I—"

"No, it's okay," he said, walking away. "You've got things to do—and so do I."

"You'll call me?"

"Sure," he said. "First chance I get."

But then he stopped and turned back to her. "One other thing," he said. "I want you to let me know."

"Let you know what?"

"If you're pregnant. I'm not like your old man."

"Meaning what, Ben? Do you think I'm like my white mother? Do you think if I were pregnant, I'd try to find some way to get rid of it?"

He stood for a moment, then came back to her, putting his good arm around her and holding her tightly. She clung to him, her face hidden in his shirtfront.

"I'm sorry," he whispered against her ear, his hand stroking her cropped-off hair. "I promised myself I wouldn't do this—I wouldn't try to keep you—or make it hard for you—when you wanted to go—"

I don't want to go, she almost said, but Lucas Singer was impatiently waiting and this wasn't the time.

He made her look at him. "I will call you."

Lucas blew the horn sharply.

"I think that's for me," Ben said. He stood there for a moment longer, and he was about to say something else, but Lucas leaned on the horn again.

"Will you go before he takes a stick to you?" Eden said, and he laughed.

"Ben," she called when he was about to get into the police vehicle. "Please be careful." She didn't mean just in the line of duty; she meant in the meeting with Becenti, but she couldn't say that.

He gave her a half smile and a wave. She stood watching until Lucas Singer pulled the police vehicle around and drove away.

The name of the game, Toomey thought, was How Many Times Can You Tell the Same Story the Same Way?

As many times as you want, Captain—Lieutenant—

He was exhausted by the constant questions. He must have related the events that led up to the shooting a hundred times now. There was nothing, *nothing,* he could have done to prevent it, and he resented the insinuation that he could. The man with the shotgun hadn't been caught in between the roadblocks; he'd come from the opposite direction. He had stopped his vehicle, and as Toomey approached to advise him that he couldn't continue, he had abruptly fired. There had been no warning, no confrontation, no indication of any kind that it was open season on tribal cops. Nothing. Toomey had been wounded first; Joey had come running. And Joey got the other barrel pointblank.

The phone on Becenti's desk buzzed. Toomey focused on not listening to the conversation—which led to the inevitable—the memory of Eden, standing there with her little-boy haircut and her beautiful eyes and his too-big sweatshirt.

He had hurt her with his pregnancy remark. He knew that, because he had seen the look before. He had caused the look before. He didn't know what made him say it— yes, he did. He said it because he thought he was being dismissed. After the night they had spent together, it was suddenly Thank-you-for-your-services-I-have-to-run-along-now. He didn't know what he had expected when he had been so tactless and to the point.

I want you to come to bed with me.

And he'd gotten exactly what he asked for. Sex. Not love. Not even like. He had no idea if she would be waiting when he got finished here—if he got finished here.

He was very much afraid now that he loved her. He wasn't sure when or how it happened. He certainly didn't know why. It was something that simply *was,* like blue sky and red rock monoliths. His mother hadn't been wrong. He did want to keep Eden Trevoy. He wanted to marry her. He wanted to build a place for them to live with their many children. He wanted to look after her sheep.

The idea of Eden having a herd of sheep almost made him smile.

Almost.

So now what? Where was the harmony in this? It made no sense to him that he should feel the way he did about a woman who was so entirely wrong for him. Eden was already trying to leave, to go back to her real life of money and banks and lunches at Étienne's. She was every bit as elusive as he'd thought she would be. Capricious as the wind. Warm and loving one minute, anxious to be gone the next. Even without Lucas Singer's input, he had known that trying to hold on to somebody like her would be like trying to hold on to his own shadow. He had wanted a memory of her to keep always, and now he had one. He had only to close his eyes and he could still feel her body against his, around his. He could taste her mouth. He could smell her soft woman smell. He could remember everything.

Everything.

The very thought of her made him ache inside—

"Toomey, are you paying attention?" Becenti asked.

"No, sir," he said truthfully.

"Well, suppose you do. I don't think you realize how serious this is."

"No, sir, I don't," Toomey said. "I've told you what happened, and it's in my report. I don't know why we keep going over the same ground here. I don't think I could have done anything differently. If you do, you're going to have to tell me."

He didn't miss the look that passed between Becenti and Lucas.

"Okay," Lucas said. "Did you and Joey have some kind of argument right before all this went down?"

"No, sir."

"You're lying, Toomey—"

"No, sir, I'm not! You know what Joey's like. He's like this big—overgrown—puppy. He's never met a stranger in his whole life. You couldn't argue with him if you wanted to. Who said we had an argument?"

"He did," Lucas said.

Toomey looked at him. Whether Joey had actually said such a thing or not, there was no doubt that Lucas Singer believed it.

"What? You think we got into a fight and *I* shot him?" Toomey said. "Is that it?"

"No, that's not it," Becenti said, holding up his hand to keep Lucas from answering. "We're just trying to get at the truth."

"I've told you the truth, sir."

"Then you and Joey didn't have some kind of discussion about the Trevoy woman," Lucas said.

"What has Eden got to do with this!"

"Before they airlifted Joey out, he asked me to tell you he was sorry for what he said about Eden Trevoy," Lucas said. "Now, do you want to explain that?"

"There's nothing to explain," Toomey said.

Both men stared at him.

"There's nothing to explain!" he said.

"So you didn't even talk about her," Becenti said.

"Yes, we talked about her."

"And?"

"And that conversation is none of your business—sir," he added. "What happened to Joey and me has got nothing to do with Eden. Nothing.'' He looked at Lucas. ''If *her* name hadn't come up—if it had been somebody else's name—we wouldn't be having this meeting, would we, Lieutenant?''

Lucas didn't answer him. Toomey took a deep breath and reached deep for his self-control. He was so tired. His arm was killing him. It took him a long time to ask the question.

''Do you want my badge? Is that where we're going with this?''

''Toomey—'' Becenti began.

Someone knocked on the door. Becenti ignored it. The knock came again.

''In!'' he said finally.

Mary Skeets opened the door. ''Excuse me, sir,'' she said. ''Your wife is here.''

''I can't talk to her now,'' Becenti said.

''She doesn't want to talk to you. She's here on a legal matter.''

''What legal matter?''

''Well, she asked if Officer Toomey has legal counsel—''

Toomey looked around sharply.

''She what?'' Becenti said.

''Legal counsel,'' Mary repeated. ''And she wants to know the reason for this hearing. She wants to know right now. You know Lillian,'' Mary added.

''Yes, I know Lillian,'' Becenti said. ''Is that all?''

''Well, no, sir. She *said* that Officer Toomey had been rousted from his bed at six this morning and brought here with complete and total disregard for his obvious physical injuries and the mental trauma that resulted from having seen his fellow officer severely wounded in the line of duty—not to mention having been shot himself. She says that he was not allowed food of any kind prior to this unofficial but nevertheless illegal arrest of his person, and that, furthermore, he has been interrogated in here for hours—still without having been fed—something that neither her brother, Lieutenant Lucas Singer, nor her husband, Captain Johnny Becenti—you, sir—would tolerate happening to any other detainee in this facility—ever. And she *suggests* that something be done to remedy this grievous situation immediately—before she formally files charges of police brutality on Officer Toomey's behalf.''

''I...see,'' Becenti said, glancing at Toomey.

Toomey didn't say anything. This was just what he needed—both the captain and the lieutenant thinking he had gone running to a lawyer. Not that he could have, even if he'd wanted to. He'd been in here—with both of them—since the crack of dawn.

''You wouldn't happen to know how my wife got dragged into this, would you, Mary?''

''Actually, sir, it was my fault. Someone asked me for the name of the best 'butt-kicking' lawyer on the rez, so, naturally, I thought of Lillian.''

''Naturally,'' Becenti said. ''Who was it?''

''Who was what, sir?''

''Mary, who asked you for a lawyer?'' Becenti said pointedly.

''Oh, it was Eden Trevoy. I didn't know she was asking because of Ben. I thought it was the other thing.''

''What other thing?''

''The being Navajo thing, sir—or half Navajo. I thought maybe she wanted to try to locate her real father—her Navajo father—or something, and she wanted somebody asking the questions who wouldn't take no for an answer. You know I can't abide a man who abandons his kid—so I told her Lillian Singer-Becenti was the best there was.

And then Lillian happened to come in while Ms. Trevoy was still here—she wanted to buy you lunch, by the way—Lillian, not Ms. Trevoy—but I wouldn't count on that now, sir. You know how stirred up Lillian gets when she thinks a law enforcement agency has stepped all over somebody's civil liberties—and she's pretty stirred up at the moment. Anyway, she and Ms. Trevoy talked for a while. And then *I* got stuck with coming into the lion's den—no problem, though—all part of the job," she added with a smile.

Toomey got up out of his chair and headed for the door.

"Where do you think you're going?" Lucas said.

"To see my lawyer," he said, and he didn't stop.

He spotted Lillian as soon as he stepped into the hall. She was carrying her and Becenti's toddler son, the one Toomey was responsible for their having made—in a manner of speaking. Good old See-Nothing-Know-Nothing Toomey, who had kept his mouth shut when it counted and given Becenti and Lillian time to know if they were in love or lust.

"I don't want a lawyer," he told her immediately. She ignored the remark completely.

"My God, look at you," she said. "Eden was right to be worried—"

"Ms. Singer—Mrs. Becenti—"

"Lillian," she interrupted.

There was no way he could call her by her given name. "I don't want a lawyer," he said instead. "I don't *need* a lawyer—"

"Yes, you do. Here, take the boy," she said, offering him the toddler, who grinned around the finger he had in his mouth. But then she immediately changed her mind. "No, I'd better take him with me. You go yell at Eden for having the good sense to get somebody to intervene on your behalf, and I'll go yell at my husband. It's *much* more effective if I'm holding our child. Well, go on," she insisted.

"I don't want a lawyer," he said yet another time.

"I understand that. Go talk to Eden, anyway."

He gave a heavy sigh. "Where is she?"

"Waiting outside. I'll find you and let you know if you're done."

He was definitely done, but he didn't say so.

He walked to the side door and stepped outside. Eden was standing in the parking lot, leaning against her car, her arms folded across her breasts and her head bowed. She didn't see him until he said her name. Her head came up sharply, and the look of relief on her face was almost enough to blunt his anger.

Almost.

He watched the welcoming smile she gave him immediately fade.

"What's wrong?" she asked, reaching out to touch his uninjured arm. He wouldn't let her.

"What's wrong? You shouldn't have gone to Lillian. That's what's wrong."

"I can afford it."

"This isn't about money, Eden! This is about my job. *My* job. You had no right to interfere and no business dragging Lillian into this."

"I think there's some kind of vendetta, Ben—because of me. You need help—"

"Whether I do or not, it's not your concern. I can handle my own problems. Me. I don't want your money or your interference. Do you understand?"

She gave a sharp sigh and looked away. "No. Not really. Lucas Singer was right, I guess." She looked at him. "I just don't get the fine points. But don't worry about it,

Toomey. I don't have to have a hogan fall on me about some things. You don't want my help. You don't want my money or my concern. I'm just the—''

He winced at the choice of words she used to describe their relationship.

''My fault,'' she said, pushing by him to get into her car. ''I just didn't quite realize it until now.''

She backed the car around without looking and drove away.

He stood for a moment, wondering if the day was going to get any worse, then he walked back toward the law enforcement building. Lucas Singer watched from his office window.

Chapter Ten

It was raining in Albuquerque, a gentle and steady "female" rain. He had been born and raised in the desert. He had never quite grasped the concept that rain was supposed to be depressing. Until now.

I want to keep you, Eden. What do you think of that?

But the only thing he kept was a vigil at Joey's bedside. Lucas Singer and his wife, Sloan, came and went, and fellow tribal police officers, and Joey's family. Toomey was there almost all the time, driving back and forth to Albuquerque as often as he could, because Joey was awake enough to recognize him and seemed to rest easier if he was there.

"You're a symbol to Joey," Sloan told him.

"Of what?" he asked, surprised because he and Joey Nez weren't best friends.

"Of hope," she said. "You were caught in the same bad situation—and you survived."

And so he kept his vigil, surrounded by pay telephones, and he never once called Eden. He assumed that she was back at home now, just as he assumed that he could find her number in the book—if he wanted. Sometimes he let himself believe that he actually could call her; the rest of the time he knew better. Once, in a moment of weakness, he did look her number up, standing in the quiet corridor outside the intensive care unit, just before daylight, turning pages in the phone book until he found it.

But that was as far as he let his vacillation take him. He didn't dial the number. It was too dispiriting just looking at it. Actually speaking to her, hearing the anticipated polite dismissal in her voice, would be more than he could handle right now, no matter how well deserved it might be. He already had Lucas Singer watching him all the time—for what exactly, Toomey didn't know. And Sloan. It was obvious that *she* felt sorry for him, when she couldn't possibly know anything about his personal problems, even with the highly developed reservation grapevine.

But he managed to hang on, at least until the afternoon that Mary Skeets arrived with way too much interest in his current mental and physical state.

"What is wrong with you, Benjamin?" she asked immediately—when she was hardly off the elevator.

"Oh, I don't know, Mary. What?" he said.

"I'm serious. What's wrong with you?" she said, and suddenly, he just couldn't take anymore.

"I've got to get out of here," he said.

"Benjamin, wait, where are you going?" she called after him, but he didn't stop. The elevator arrived for once without a long wait, and he got on, catching a last glimpse of Mary's worried face as the doors closed.

He left the hospital and got into his pickup truck, and

he drove aimlessly around until he found himself on Central Avenue. He abruptly pulled into the first motel parking lot that had a pay telephone. And he kept calling banks until he found the one where Eden worked. He didn't wait on the line to talk to her. He drove there instead, and he didn't think about the advisability of doing it. He just wanted to see her.

But he lost his nerve about the same time he found a parking space. He had to sit there awhile before he made any attempt to go find her. It was still raining when he finally got out of the truck, but he didn't go inside the bank. He stood there, feeling the rain on his face, filled with longing and despair.

This is crazy, he thought.

What could he possibly say to her? He was the one who had insisted that she mind her own business. And she was doing that. No one at home had heard anything from her. Not Sadie or Faye—certainly not him. And Mary Skeets would have said something if Eden had called her. There was no point trying to see Eden again. It was better to have a clean break and be done with it—

"Ben?"

He looked sharply around. Eden stood there on the sidewalk. She was wearing a gray business suit, and she had a briefcase under her arm and an umbrella over her head. She was the perfect counterpart for the corporate-looking white man who stood impatiently next to her.

"You go on," she said to the man. "I'll catch up."

"No, I can wait for you," he said, glancing at Toomey. And at his ragged jeans and his cowboy boots and his plaid flannel shirt.

"No, it's fine," Eden assured him, and he finally walked on—but he didn't like it.

She turned her attention back to Toomey, looking at him expectantly.

She is so beautiful, he thought.

Her eyes went to his still-bandaged arm, but she made no comment. She was clearly surprised to find him here, almost as surprised as he was himself.

"So," he said finally. "This is what an investment banker looks like. I didn't recognize you at first."

She smiled. "It's the hair."

He almost smiled in return.

"How is Joey?" she asked. "He's not worse—or—"

"No. No, he's still in intensive care, but he's awake now—and talking. He says he wants to go out to the airport. He wants to see what happens when the two of us try to make it through the metal detector."

She laughed softly. "He must be better if he's making jokes."

"I guess. Sometimes he seems to know what's going on. Sometimes he doesn't. Last night he kept talking about a picture he thought I had in my desk at the law enforcement building."

"What kind of picture?"

"A picture of you."

He finally let his eyes meet hers.

"He thought I had a picture of you—and I couldn't talk him out of it."

The conversation lagged. He looked past her. The "suit" hadn't gone very far, and he looked pointedly at his watch.

"Do you want to go get something to eat?" Eden asked abruptly. "I haven't had lunch. We could have an early dinner. I owe you one."

"No," he said.

"No," she repeated. She took a deep breath. "Ben, what are you doing here?"

"The truth? I thought maybe we could go back to the way we were before—when you were staying with Sadie and learning about the People. Friends, you know? But I can't do it. I can't pretend nothing happened between us. I can't pretend that it didn't mean anything to me. I don't know what to say to you. I don't know how I'm supposed to behave, so I act like I don't care. I'm afraid of what I feel, and I end up hurting you when I don't mean to. I—"

"Eden!" the "suit" called. "We're going to be late! Let's go!"

She didn't answer him.

"Eden!" he yelled.

"In a minute, Harrison!" she said.

"There's no cure for this, is there?" Toomey said.

"No," she said, her voice barely a whisper. She looked at him for a long moment, her eyes lingering on his face. He thought that she was going to cry.

But she turned abruptly and walked away.

"So who is he?"

"Benjamin Toomey," Eden said, lowering her umbrella and switching it to her other hand so she could open the door.

"I repeat," Harrison said. "Who is he?"

She didn't reply because she honestly didn't know the answer to that question.

"What? You're not going to tell me?" Harrison persisted as they walked across the cavernous bank lobby. "Let me guess. You're...jacking up his portfolio." He grinned at her, clearly impressed by his own wit.

Eden stopped walking and looked him directly in the eyes. "He's the love of my life, Harrison," she said quietly, because she wanted—needed—to tell someone, and Harrison's approval or disapproval didn't really matter.

"Yeah, right," he answered, laughing because he was so sure she had just made a joke. He kept expecting her to join in, to share the immense humor in this.

She stepped around him and walked on.

"You *were* kidding?" he said, catching up.

She gave him a look, but she didn't answer.

"No, really," he said. "You were kidding."

"No," she said.

"But he's—"

"He's what, Harrison?" she asked when he didn't go on.

"He's...not an investment banker."

"No. He's a police officer."

"Is that where the bandages came from?"

"Yes. He was shot in the line of duty. The officer who was with him is still in intensive care at the medical center."

"Yeah? That's too bad. So what's the problem? I know there is one—you've both got that look. There *is* a problem, right?"

Once again, she didn't answer him, but he was undeterred.

"What is it?" he said. "Your family thinks he's not good enough for you?"

"No, his family thinks *I'm* not good enough for *him*."

"Well, damn, Eden. That's a tough one."

"But the *real* problem, Harrison, is that they are absolutely right."

She went into her office and shut the door on whatever else Harrison intended to say. She had meetings all afternoon, important ones that she couldn't miss or even be late for. She sat down at her desk and stared at nothing. Everything had changed. *She* had changed. A few weeks ago, she was one of the best in the business. Her co-workers stood in line for her latest financial insights. Now she'd lost her edge, because she simply didn't care. There were too many other things to think about, things like sunsets and moonlight, butterflies and flowers and grass, things she had hardly even noticed before. Mother Earth. Father Sky. She should have never gone and stayed with Sadie Benally; she wouldn't have if she had known what raising one's consciousness really meant.

She sighed heavily and picked up her briefcase. Living with Sadie wasn't the cause of her transformation. Loving Sadie's grandson was.

Oh, Ben. What are we going to do?

She had to force herself to go into the first meeting. She sat there at the big mahogany table, and she tried to pay attention, tried to maintain some semblance of her old "wunderkind" self until it was over. But between meetings, she called the medical center for the number of the pay phone in the intensive care unit waiting area, and she dialed it before she lost her nerve. Mary Skeets answered almost immediately.

"What a surprise!" Mary said as soon as Eden identified herself. "How are you?"

"Fine, Mary. I was wondering if—"

"He's not here."

"I beg your pardon?" Eden said, taken aback.

"You're looking for Ben, right?"

"Well—yes."

"He just left. He's gone home."

"Oh, I see," she said, hoping she didn't sound as disappointed as she felt. "Thanks, Mary. Nice talking to you."

"Eden," Mary said when she was about to hang up. "You know where he lives."

She didn't say anything.

"It's Friday and you probably don't have to work tomorrow. Do you?" Mary asked pointedly.

"No, but I—"

"Ben could use some cheering up. He is *really* down."

"Mary—"

"He needs *you* to cheer him up, Eden."

"I think that would cause him more problems than he already has."

"Well—you know best, I guess," Mary said. "Think about it. He's a good guy."

Eden didn't want to think about it. She couldn't go looking for Ben. The idea here was to not complicate his life. As angry as she had been with Lucas Singer at the time, on some level she had agreed with him. She wasn't good for Ben Toomey. How could she be when she understood so little about his life and his beliefs and so little about him?

He came looking for me—

"Eden, they're ready to start!" Harrison whispered loudly, waving at her frantically from down the hall.

She hung up the phone and walked in his direction.

No, she thought halfway there. *No.*

"Eden, where are you going?"

"I'm not feeling well, Harrison," she called over her shoulder. "I have to go home."

She didn't tell him that "home" was a person.

It rained all the way to Gallup, and then to Window Rock. It was still raining when she turned down the rutted road to Ben's place. She saw immediately that the trailer was dark and that his truck wasn't there. Mary had been mistaken. He hadn't gone home—unless he was at Sadie's or unless "home" was a person for him, too.

The rain came down harder; the wind buffeted against the car. She was tired from the drive, and she propped her arms on the steering wheel and rested her head on them.

Now what?

At least she could save face. He wouldn't even have to know she'd been here.

She sat up, and she was about to back the car around. But then she realized that the trailer door was open and that Ben stood there watching. He made no attempt to stop her from leaving; he simply waited, the door held wide.

She stared at him through the rain-splattered window, then cut off the motor and opened the car door. She got out and began to walk steadily in his direction. The rain beat down on her and the wind whipped at her clothes. Her high heels mired in the mud. She bent down to pull one of her shoes back on. When she looked up, Ben had come outside on the stoop.

She walked the rest of the way to him, and she stopped on the step just below where he stood.

"Are you lost?" he asked.

"Yes," she answered. There was a tremor in her voice she couldn't do anything about.

"Me, too," he said.

He held out his hand, and she immediately took it, letting him bring her inside. She stood shivering while he switched on a small lamp. She kicked off her muddy shoes just inside the door, and when he reached for her and his arms went around her, she couldn't keep from making a small, needy sound.

Home, she thought, clinging to him hard. She loved the way he smelled. She loved the way he felt.

"I don't know what's happening," she said. She leaned back to see his face, her eyes searching his. "I don't—"

She was about to cry and she pressed her face into his chest again. His warm hand stroked her cheek.

"Maybe this—right now—is all there is for us," he said. "Maybe we can't have anything else."

"Then we'll have to take what we can," she said. She wanted no promises from him, and she had no expectations about what might happen in the future. She had never had much luck with expectations. By necessity, she had convinced herself that she was happy being alone, answering to no one, and that her Edna-imposed solitary state was not the same as being lonely. She had convinced herself that she was past that. But she had been lonely all her life, would still be lonely if it weren't for Ben Toomey, and she would be happy with whatever he could give. She lifted her mouth to his. He kissed her lips, her eyes and her lips again.

"Don't cry," he whispered. "Don't—"

She tried to do as he asked; she made no sound, and yet the tears ran down her face in spite of all she could do.

"Do you want to talk?" he asked.

"No. I want—"

"What?" he asked when she didn't go on.

"You. I want you—"

His arms tightened around her for a moment, and then he stepped away from her and led her by the hand into the bedroom. He switched on the reading lamp, and he stood there looking at her. Just…looking.

"I don't know this woman," he said, reaching to touch her lapel. "The banker in the wet power suit."

"It's still me," she said. She wiped at the tears with the back of her hand.

He helped her off with her wet jacket and hung it up

for her. Then he went away and came back with a towel. He dried her face and her hair with it and gently wiped away her tears again.

When she reached for the buttons on her blouse, he caught her hands.

"Let me do it," he said. He gave her a slightly mischievous smile. "My fantasy this time."

She stood quietly, looking into his face as he undid her blouse, memorizing every expression, every nuance. He was in no hurry, pausing from time to time to gently stroke her bared skin. She could feel his desire in the slight tremor of his hands, see it in his eyes. He liked what he saw and touched and tasted, and she reveled in it.

He took her blouse away, gently enfolded her in his arms again and pressed her body against his. He held her close, his breath warm against her neck.

In spite of all she could do, she was crying again. He moved so that he could see her face.

"What is it? Tell me."

She shook her head.

"Tell me," he said again.

She took a small wavering breath. "You...love me," she said. "I can feel it."

"Yes," he answered.

My poor Ben, she thought, and she wrapped her arms around him as if she would never let go. It wasn't his loving her that made her weep. It was that his loving her made him so unhappy. She could feel that, too, in the midst of his longing, and it broke her heart that she was bringing him such misery when she only wanted to bring him joy.

She kissed his cheek and then the corner of his mouth and his eyes.

"I love you," she whispered. "I love you, Ben."

She kissed his lips then, seeking, needing everything he could give. His hands slid into her hair.

And suddenly there was no more time. Time had become the enemy. They had to have each other now, before it was too late, before something, before someone came between them. She helped take off the rest of her clothes and his, and she lay down on the bed, her arms outstretched. Eager for each other, their bodies slid together, heart to heart, skin to skin. She couldn't hold him close enough. There was nothing more to be said; there was only the wanting. His hands, his mouth sought her breasts. Desire tore through her. His touch was so strong and sure. She strained to have more. They both trembled, and when he finally entered her, she was more than ready for him. He said something against her ear, something she didn't try to understand. She was lost in the exquisite sensation of having him again. Nothing else mattered. Her body rose to meet his, striving to give, to take.

The love of my life, she thought in the last moments. *I love you, Ben!*

Chapter Eleven

He lay listening to the rain and to her quiet breathing. She had actually said the words.

I love you.

He should be the happiest man on this earth—Eden Trevoy *loved* him—but he wasn't. He knew only too well that that small miracle would only make it harder for them both. He wondered how much time they had before she went back to Albuquerque. It would have to be soon. She had her job there, the one that paid her twice the money he would ever make, money she didn't even need because of her trust fund.

We have to take what we can.

Last night and in the heat of passion, that had seemed enough. Now he wasn't nearly so willing to just make do. He still wanted a life with her. He still wanted all those simple mundane things. Marriage. Children. Living and growing old together like the old couple who had first owned the trailer.

He gave a quiet sigh. He had to go in to work by seven, and all he wanted was to stay here with her. Make love and sleep and make love again. He would never get enough of her. Never.

He closed his eyes and tightened his arms around her. She stirred slightly, her hand coming up to briefly touch his face.

This is what I want, he thought. *This.*

He opened his eyes again at the sound of a vehicle. Faye, bringing his truck back after an evening of hauling her giggly girlfriends to all the line-dance places they could find between here and Albuquerque. He forced himself to get up and put on his jeans. Faye would know exactly whose car was parked in the yard, and she would ask her many questions, anyway.

But by the time he opened the trailer door, whoever had brought his truck had gone.

Not Faye, then, he thought. Someone in authority, someone who thought now was not the time to talk about Eden Trevoy being here or to let Faye ask her questions.

He went back inside and showered and dressed. He didn't wake Eden until he was ready to leave. He sat down on the side of the bed and stroked her back until she opened her eyes.

She immediately smiled and reached for him.

"You're going?" she murmured, her fingers lightly touching his cheek. She was still more asleep than awake.

He took her hand, sliding his fingers in between hers. "Duty calls," he said. "I'm not sure how long I'll be." It took every ounce of willpower he had not to ask if she would still be here when he returned.

"Do I have to leave?" she asked, and he smiled.

"Never," he said.

"Good. I'm too...sleepy to go..."

He kissed her, several times, then pulled the blanket over her bare shoulder because the room was cold. He looked back at her one last time before he reluctantly left her there. The rain had stopped when he stepped outside. Sadie's pinto horse was in the corral, and Sadie stood waiting by his truck.

"Grandma," he said, surprised. For the first time in his life he wasn't happy to see her.

"Benjamin," she said gravely.

"Sorry, Grandma, I'm in a hurry," he said. "I have to get to work."

"I'm not here to see you, Benjamin."

He stood there, not quite looking at her, and he gave a quiet sigh.

"Eden is sleeping," he said. There was no use in pretending he didn't know what—or who—Sadie had come about.

"I'll wait," she said.

"What are you going to say to her?" he asked.

His grandmother didn't answer him.

"I love her," he said. "You—and my mother—think it's only that I need a woman. It's not that. I need *her*. I love *her*."

"Yes," Sadie answered.

"What are you going to say to her?" he asked again.

"What I have to say has nothing to do with you."

"Grandma—"

"It has nothing to do with you, Benjamin. Go be the policeman. If Eden wants you to know this business, she'll tell you."

He stood a moment longer. "I know you don't approve—"

"She doesn't know who she is, Benjamin," Sadie said. "And now maybe she can't ever know."

"What do you mean?"

"I mean that maybe you've made it so she will have to be whatever pleases you."

"She's a strong person, Grandma. She does things her own way. And I wouldn't ask her to do that."

"If she loves you, you won't have to ask. I think having somebody care about her is a new thing for her. You said it yourself. She had no relatives to teach her. If you need her, maybe she'll try to be what you need—what you think she is. But in the end, she won't be happy. A woman with no true self—how can she find the *hozro?* The harmony has to start in here," she said, touching her heart.

"I can help her find out who she is."

"No, Benjamin. I told you before. You need to stay out of the way. And she needs to be free to find the path that is right for her. It's too hard for her to make the journey if she has to worry about hurting you. She has to learn to live with the lies of all those people who should have taken care of her. All of them betrayed her—her white mother and her Navajo father, and the one who died, *she* most of all, because she sent the little girl away and paid other people to do what she should have done. How can Eden know how to trust in herself or anyone else? Maybe she can't keep from hurting you."

"She's not going to hurt me, Grandma," he said, hoping that he sounded as if he believed it.

"She will if she decides she's white and she belongs in that big glass bank."

"And if she decides she's Navajo?"

"Is that what you're hoping, Benjamin?"

He looked away without answering the question. No. He didn't hope that. He didn't dare.

Sadie moved to open his truck door and take out a bundle of clothes.

"These things belong to Eden," she said. "She left them at my house. She will need them here if you're going to keep her."

She stood there with the bundle in her arms, waiting, for what he didn't quite know. He had nothing else he wanted to say.

"There is something you need to remember, Benjamin," Sadie said.

"What is that, Grandma?"

"This young woman has a long way to go. Navajo or white. With or without you."

Eden sat in the law enforcement building parking lot, waiting for Ben to come out. His truck was still here; it was well past the time when his shift supposedly ended. She didn't know why he hadn't come out yet. She only knew why she didn't go inside to look for him—because she didn't want to have to deal with Lucas Singer.

There was a very recent time in her life when she would have made a special point of annoying someone like him, someone in authority who thought he had some dominion over the irrepressible Eden Trevoy. Ben was the one reason that she didn't do it. She didn't want her behavior to cause him any more problems than it already had, not when the simple fact of her existence had caused him difficulty enough. But it wasn't easy to behave. She was still the refractory rich girl, dedicated to having her own way. The old arrogance was very much in evidence. It hadn't disappeared along with her lost identity. There was something to be said for the "take no prisoners" mentality. It kept the fears at bay—most of the time. It kept one from feeling so vulnerable—and cowering in a parking lot.

"Are you looking for Toomey?"

She hadn't known anyone was nearby, and the suddenness of the question made her jump. She looked around to see who asked, and she gave a heavy sigh.

Lucas Singer himself.

She was so *tired* of this man. She braced herself for yet another of their encounters.

"Yes, I am," she said. "But I'm not going disrupt your...police business."

"He's not here," Lucas said, clearly ignoring her sarcasm.

"I don't suppose you're going to tell me where he might be?"

"He's out on a call. I don't know when he'll get back."

"And you wouldn't tell me if you did."

He didn't answer her, didn't say anything else. She glanced at him, wondering why he was still standing there peering into her open car window.

"Is there...anything I can help you with?" he asked after a moment.

"You mean like a bus ticket out of town?"

"No, I mean like finding Billy George."

"How did you know I was looking for Billy George?"

"Sadie Benally came by here. She said he wasn't at his place and she needed to locate him—for you."

"Do you know where he is?"

"Yes. He's sick. He's staying at a sheep camp with one of his daughters."

"Will you tell me how to get there?"

"No," he said.

"What is it with you!" she said, hitting the steering wheel with her fist. "I don't understand what your problem is!"

"I can't tell you how to get there, Ms. Trevoy. There

are no directions and no landmarks. You have to just know where you're going."

She stared at him, trying to decide if she believed him or not.

"Look," he said finally. "You can't get there by yourself. I'm shorthanded, with Toomey hurt and Joey Nez in the hospital, and I don't have anybody who can take you there. I certainly don't have anybody to send looking for you when you get lost. But—" he said, holding up his hand when she was about to interrupt. "If you want, I'll see if I can work something out for you."

"Why?" she asked pointedly. "Why would you do that?"

He didn't pretend that he didn't understand the reason behind the question. "Because I raised a boy who was half Navajo. I know how hard it was for him to find a place where he fit. I think I can guess how hard it is for you—especially if you didn't know about your heritage until now. Sadie Benally thinks you should talk to Billy George—and you do, too, apparently. He's an old man and he's not well. Now do you want my help or do you want to waste time arguing about it?"

She sat there. "Does everybody around here know my business?" she asked after a moment.

"Sooner or later," he said. He opened the car door as if she had already accepted his offer.

She sighed. "Okay," she said, getting out. "If you can work something out, I would appreciate it."

She followed him into the building, and she didn't miss Mary Skeets's startled look when Eden and Lucas Singer walked in together.

"I'm going to check with my wife," Lucas said. "She's a nurse practitioner at the clinic—"

"We've met," Eden said.

"It may be that some of the medical team is going out there to check on Billy, and you could ride along with one of them."

Eden waited while he went to see. It was taking a long time.

"Mary," Eden said. "Do you think I could leave a note on Ben's desk?"

"Don't see why not," Mary said. "Well, I do see why not, but you and Lucas seem to be on speaking terms to-day. Ben's desk is through there. It's the one that looks like it's been thrown in front of a herd of stampeding elephants. The one over by the file cabinets."

"I should be able to find that," Eden assured her.

Locating the desk was no problem. Locating a pen or pencil to write with was something else again. She hesitated, then opened the middle drawer. She found a stub of a pencil immediately—and a damaged color snapshot of a young woman. Mary came through with a handful of While You Were Out slips to distribute to the various desktops. She reached over Eden's shoulder to put two of them on Ben's desk.

"Who's that?" Mary asked, because the drawer was still open and the photograph was clearly visible.

And because Mary was Mary.

"I don't know," Eden said. "I think this must be the picture Joey was confused about. Ben said Joey thought there was one of me in his desk and he couldn't talk him out of it. I guess people get things mixed up when they've been hurt."

"Let me see," Mary said, taking it out. "Well, she does look a little bit like you—especially since you got your hair cut and people can see your face. Joey wasn't that far off the beam—oh, no. I just realized who this is—"

"Who?" Eden said.

Mary didn't answer. She stared at the snapshot.

"Mary, I need you!" Lucas Singer yelled from the hall.

"Oh, no," Mary said again, shoving the snapshot at Eden. "Here comes Lucas. Get rid of it."

"Mary, what—"

"Get rid of it! You do *not* want Lucas to see that!"

"Why?"

"Just do it!" Mary said, whispering now.

But it was too late. Eden had the photograph in her hand, and she couldn't drop it into the drawer without Lucas seeing her do it. He looked from one of them to the other, his eyes finally resting on the snapshot.

"Oops! Look at the time!" Mary said, glancing at her watch and scurrying away.

"What are you doing?" Lucas said.

"Leaving Ben a note," Eden answered.

"Besides that," he said.

Eden took a small breath and looked up at him. "I'm trying to keep you from seeing this photograph. Why, I have no idea."

He took it out of her hand. He hardly glanced at it, but there was a flicker of something in his face when he looked at it—pain, Eden would have said if she had had to identify it. He put the photograph into his shirt pocket.

"That was in Ben's desk," Eden protested, because she didn't think he should keep it.

"It belongs to me," he said. "Leave your note. I've made arrangements for you to talk to Billy."

"When?"

"Now."

She looked at him for a moment, then hastily scribbled a few words on a sheet of paper, telling Ben that she was going to try to talk to Billy George and that she had no idea when she would return.

"Do you want to read it?" she asked Lucas when she finished.

"That won't be necessary," he said. "Let's go."

"Where are we going?"

"My wife is already in the area making some house calls. She's on her way to Billy's daughter's place—eventually. We're going to try to catch up with her."

"We?" Eden asked, not far from incredulous. "You're going?"

"You know how it is, Ms. Trevoy. There's no one any more nonessential than middle management."

"Oh, I know that. I just don't know why you'd put yourself out like this—given our previous conversations," she said as they walked outside.

"I feel sorry for you," he said.

"*You* feel sorry for *me*," she repeated.

"I told you. I raised a boy who was half Navajo."

"You've been trying to make me stay away from Ben."

"I still am," he said. He unlocked the door to the police vehicle and opened it for her to get in.

She looked at him for a moment. "Well," she said. "As long as we know where we stand.

"This...boy you raised," she said when they were on the road. "He was your son?"

"No. He's my wife's nephew. My nephew by marriage. Sloan's brother was his father. He died when the boy was three. His mother was a Navajo woman named Margaret Madman. She wasn't fit to raise him and she wanted Sloan to take him. There were a lot of legal difficulties for a while. Sloan was the only person who wanted him, but she was white and the child had to be raised Navajo. When we got married, the boy and his half brother and half sister became my family."

"The half siblings—they were Navajo, too?"

"No."

"But they became *your* family?"

"Yes."

"Where is the boy now?"

"Here. On the rez. He's studying to be a *hataalii*. A *hataalii* is—"

"I know what a *hataalii* is."

"Sadie Benally taught you about healers, medicine men?"

"Yes."

"She's taught you a lot about the People."

"Yes."

"Like what?"

"Oh, plants and herbs. What heals what. And procedures—how things are done."

"What kind of procedures?"

"Ones for living—for walking in beauty—and for getting along with other people. What to do if you owe me money and you don't pay me back, or if you walk off with some of my sheep mixed in with yours. The right way to voice a grievance. Things like that."

"Professor Trevoy knew about the Old Ones. What did you learn from her?"

"Nothing—except how to get along by myself," she said. "At the country club, of course. Only now I pay my own dues." She looked at him and smiled, pleased to have him know that this new civility of his didn't fool her. She already knew his opinion of her, just as she knew that it hadn't changed.

They rode for a long time in silence.

"Do you know what's wrong with Billy George?" she asked. They were on a dirt road now—or what might pass for a dirt road. The police vehicle bounced along; Eden had to hold on to the door, in spite of her seat belt.

"He's had another heart attack—and he won't stay in the hospital."

"Do you think he'll talk to me?"

"No, I think he'll talk to me."

"Do you know what to ask him?"

"I'll ask him if he thinks it's going to rain. And if he's had any trouble with coyotes. And how his grandchildren and his sheep are. Then I'll make him laugh a little by telling him I think he's still hauling water. When he was a younger man, he was one of the most notorious bootleggers in these parts. The tribal police and the ATF never did catch him. Then, I'll give him a chance to annoy me with a few friendly insults about police incompetency. After that, if nobody brings up anything else, I'll ask him what he knows about your adoption."

"I'd rather ask him myself."

"You can't. He doesn't speak English well enough."

"You mean he won't speak English well enough."

"Same difference," Lucas said. "The old man understands English, but he's not going to use it."

"I still don't know why you're doing this," she said, more to herself than to him.

"I told you why."

"Oh, that's right. You feel *sorry* for me."

"Yes. And I feel sorry for the tribe—the People. We don't like having our children taken away. If one of them belongs here, even one brought up to be as indifferent as you are, we need to know about it. And this could be the only chance you have, Ms. Trevoy, to find out what *you* want to know. Billy George is sick and old. When he's gone, there may be no one else to ask. Of course, that might suit you better. Then you can forget the whole thing—go back to Albuquerque and the country club. And nobody there would ever have to know anything about Professor Trevoy's little arrangement."

"Which would certainly make *you* happy," she said.

"Like you said. As long as we know where we stand."

He didn't say anything else and neither did she. She watched the passing scenery and hung on to the door. When they finally arrived at the sheep camp where Billy George was staying, there was no sign of Lucas Singer's wife having arrived.

"We won't wait for Sloan. You still want to do this?" Lucas said before he got out of the police vehicle.

She looked at him. "Yes," she said, knowing it was a lie. She didn't want to do this at all. It wasn't so much that she didn't want to know. It was that she was afraid to know, and yet she couldn't help herself.

She opened the vehicle door to get out.

"Stay here," Lucas said.

"I'm not going to barge up to the door, Lieutenant. I know how it's done," Eden said.

She climbed out of the vehicle and jumped to the ground, dodging the dogs that milled about. She could hear the bleating of sheep somewhere in the distance. The place was similar to the Toomey-Benally compound; there was a traditional hogan, but there was only one—or perhaps two—residences. After a time, a woman appeared at the door of the small white prefab house. The recent rain had splattered mud on the outside walls nearly to the bottoms of the windows. The dogs gave a belated bark or two, escorted Lucas partway to the door, then went back to eating their supper out of an upturned garbage can lid.

Eden watched from a polite distance. Lucas did all the talking, speaking with a mixture of Navajo and English words and with his hands, frequently jabbing the air with his fingers widespread, once turning and making the same gesture in Eden's direction.

The woman went back inside, returning after a moment to invite them both in. Eden immediately recognized her intent and was already walking forward when Lucas Singer summoned her.

The inside of the house was pleasantly warm and smelled of hot coffee. Billy George lay in a large green vinyl recliner off to one side of the living room. The woman—Billy's daughter, Eden supposed—immediately brought two kitchen chairs for her and Lucas Singer to sit on. And Eden didn't miss the look Lucas gave her, the same look one would use to forewarn a child of the dire consequences of misbehaving.

Eden gave a quiet sigh and sat down. And waited. It was a good thing Lucas had advised her of the circuitous route he would take to get to the matter of her adoption, because it was a long, *long* time before she sensed that the conversation had turned to that. She knew the precise moment when the question was posed, because it was the only time Billy George looked directly at her and because of the long silence that followed.

Eden tried to respect the silence and couldn't.

"I want you to translate everything he says," she said to Lucas.

"He hasn't said anything, Ms. Trevoy."

"If he does, I want to know what it is right now—as we go along. I don't want you trying to remember what he said later."

Lucas didn't agree or disagree, but when Billy finally spoke, he immediately repeated it in English. The old man's voice was as feeble as he himself seemed to be, brittle and dry as the desert wind.

"Billy says it was a long time ago and he doesn't remember much anymore. He wants to know how it is you came here to see him.''

''Tell him,'' she said, not quite looking at the old man, ''Sadie Benally said I should ask Billy George about this—because he used to work for...for the one who died. Tell him that I have no relatives, no family, no one else I can ask. Say I would be grateful for anything he could recall. And, Lieutenant Singer, please do it as if you were asking on behalf of the half-Navajo boy you raised.''

Lucas frowned, but he spoke to Billy, and the old man replied.

''He says he thinks it's better to let these things alone. He says he remembers Follows-like-a-Lamb when she was a little girl, and he doesn't want to bring her sorrow.''

''Tell him I already have the sorrow—because I don't know who I am or where I belong. It may be that what he knows will take some of that sorrow away. But whether it does or not, I won't blame him for telling me the truth. I already know that my Navajo father and my white mother didn't want me.''

Billy's daughter brought in three cups of coffee while Lucas was translating, offering each of them one. Eden thanked her and held the cup tightly in her cold hands, her head bowed as she waited, trying to look more patient than she felt. Her mind went to Ben. She wished he had come here with her. She was afraid still, and he was the only person she knew would understand. He had wanted her to learn about being Navajo. Perhaps she was about to learn too much.

She looked up as the old man began to speak. Lucas followed immediately with the translation.

''Billy says that there was a white man who used to come to the ruins to visit the one who died. He thinks that this man was a person 'who pushes words out'—a lawyer—and he thinks that maybe the two of them were lovers, but he isn't sure.

"He says one time, when the man came, he was upset—no *hozro*—his harmony was gone. The man was very worried about someone he knew—someone who was about to make a bad mistake. He told the one who died that there was going to be a baby and that the mother—didn't want it. He said he was afraid that this woman would want to get rid of the baby, and if she did, it would ruin her life—because she was always doing wrong things to spite her family and then regretting them later. The man said he wished he could find someone to take the baby for her, so she wouldn't do another wrong thing. He said he had asked some people, but he couldn't find anyone who would agree without seeing the baby first—because it would be a half-breed. And the woman—she didn't want any record, any way her people would know she had this child.

"Then the one who died said, 'Tell her I'll take it,' but the man—he didn't believe her. So the one who died said it again. And again. 'I'll take this baby,' she said. And she said she would sign all the papers. She would keep the secret. She would agree to whatever the woman wanted.

"Billy says he thinks Follows-like-a-Lamb was this child. He thinks the mother was somebody who was like the one who died—someone who came from far away on an airplane to study the People. Billy says the man told her, 'You poke your nose into the business of people who are dead and she pokes her nose into the business of people who are alive—and both of you forget that you are not welcome here.'"

Billy abruptly stopped talking and sipped his coffee. It was all Eden could do not to prompt him for more information. She sat there, trying to make sense of what he had said. This woman—her real mother—had been "like"

Edna. Someone who studied the Anasazi? No, Billy said "people who are alive." An anthropologist, then? Someone from the academic community? Perhaps someone Edna already knew. Perhaps Eden herself had actually met her at some point, this impulsive woman who hadn't wanted her misbegotten child.

"The man," Eden said, causing both Lucas and Billy George to look at her. Her voice sounded strained and on the verge of tears, but she couldn't help it. Hearing the details of her adoption—even in such meager detail—was far more painful that she realized it would be. "The man," she said again, trying to make her voice stronger. "This lawyer. Does Billy know his name?"

Lucas asked the question, and Billy answered.

"He says no. He can't remember now."

"Can he tell me what he looked like—?"

"He says he can't remember anything about him."

"Was the man tall, short? Fat, skinny?"

"He says it's too long ago," Lucas said without bothering to translate any of her questions.

"Then does he have any idea who the Navajo man was?" Eden persisted. She couldn't bring herself to identify him as "my father." Whatever else he may have been, he was never that. "Did Billy ever hear any rumors about him?"

This time Lucas deigned to ask the old man the question, but Billy George didn't answer. He closed his eyes instead, holding the coffee cup precariously in his hands.

"He is very tired," his daughter said, coming in and taking away the cup. "Please don't ask him anything else."

Eden sighed and stood up, unwilling to let go of this so soon. But Billy George appeared to be sleeping. There was nothing for her to do but leave.

"When he wakes," she said to his daughter. "Will you tell him that I thank him for his help?"

His daughter nodded.

"If he should happen to remember anything else, could you let me know, maybe leave a message with Mary Skeets at the law enforcement building in Window Rock?"

"Yes," his daughter said. "You should find your father. You should find where you belong."

"Thank you—for your kindness and for your hospitality," Eden said, giving her back the coffee cup.

When she turned to go, Billy George opened his eyes again and said something, motioning for Lucas to come closer. His voice was very faint, and Lucas had to bend down to hear him. Eden stood watching as Lucas listened intently to whatever the old man tried to say.

But suddenly Lucas straightened and attempted to move away. Billy reached out and caught his arm to keep him there, still talking. Lucas clearly didn't want to hear any more. He pulled his arm free and headed for the door, sidestepping both Eden and Billy's daughter to get out.

"Lucas Singer—" Billy called after him, trying to raise up on one elbow.

"*N'dah!*" Lucas answered, without looking back and without stopping.

The only Navajo word Eden understood.

No.

She looked at the old man. For one brief moment their eyes met. The sadness, the pity she saw in them struck her as if it had been a physical blow. She turned abruptly and followed Lucas outside.

"Lieutenant—"

"Get in the vehicle, Ms. Trevoy," he said.

"But—"

"The visit is over. Even you should be able to tell that."

She stood for a moment longer, then opened the door

on the passenger side and got in. Lucas started the motor immediately and backed out of the yard. She had to buckle her seat belt as the vehicle bumped and bounced down the so-called road. She kept looking at him. The sun was going down; she could barely see his features. But she didn't miss the grim set of his jaw and his hands clenched tightly on the steering wheel. She sat there, trying to be reasonable, trying to let go of her apprehension.

It was nothing, she kept telling herself. My imagination. And all the while she knew better. She had Edna to blame for that, Edna who had "protected" her by never saying when she was leaving and letting Eden wake up time and time again to find her gone. Eden *knew* when something was being kept from her. She could feel it as surely as she could stick her hand under a running faucet and feel the water on her fingers. Whatever Billy George had said had been clearly upsetting—and it had been about her.

They rode back to Window Rock in silence, and when they reached the law enforcement building, Lucas gave her no time to ask any questions. He immediately got out and strode away.

But she wasn't about to be put off. She pushed open the door and followed after him, nearly running to catch up.

"I want to know what Billy George said," she said, trying to get in front of him so she could see his face.

Lucas didn't answer her.

"Lieutenant! Tell me what he said!" she insisted.

"Nothing. Go home, Ms. Trevoy—"

"You're not telling me the truth!" she cried. "You said you understood—because you raised that half-Navajo boy! I want—*I need*—to know what Billy George said to you!"

"What's going on?"

Eden looked around sharply at the sound of Ben's voice. She hadn't even noticed him standing there.

"Take your woman home," Lucas said to him, trying to get by her.

"I want to know what he said to you!" Eden cried, grabbing on to Lucas's arm.

He ignored her completely. "Take your woman home, Toomey! Right now!" He pulled his arm free and walked on.

"Please—" Eden said, but he chose not to hear her. "Please!" she said again, she, who never said "please" to anyone. She would have followed him right into the building if Ben hadn't caught her and held her back.

"Eden—what are you doing!"

"He won't tell me! He knows something and he won't tell me!" she said, struggling to get out of his grasp.

"Stop! Eden! You aren't going to get anywhere like this! You aren't going to get anywhere like this," he repeated when she finally looked at him. She sagged against him, and he put his arms around her and held her tight. People who came and went in the parking lot stared at them curiously.

"Take it easy, okay?" he said.

"No," she said into his shirt. "I don't want to take it easy. I didn't ask for any of this, Ben—"

"Now is not the time. You're not going to make Lucas tell you anything he doesn't want to tell you. Do you understand?"

"No—"

"Come on. Let's go."

"I have to find out about this, Ben!"

"Not now, Eden. I mean it."

She closed her eyes, her hand clutching at his shirt, her mind racing to find alternatives. She could go back and talk to Billy George—if she could find the sheep camp again. His daughter spoke English. She had seemed sympathetic—

"Eden," Ben said, trying to make her look at him.

"You go on," she said. "I don't want you to get in trouble. This is between me and Lucas Singer."

"What do you think you're going to do? Beat it out of him?"

"I don't know what I'm going to do! I just know that I can't let it go. Billy George said something to him. About me. I want to know what it is."

"Eden—"

"Ben, will you just go on home!"

"No, damn it! I won't. I love you—I'm not going to leave you here."

"Ben, please."

"No! If you want to talk to Lucas again, then we'll wait—out here—where he can't have you arrested for disturbing the peace. Okay?"

She didn't answer him, because she didn't trust her voice.

"Okay?" he said again.

"Okay," she said. She rested her head against his chest for a moment. "Thank you—" She gave a long wavering sigh. "How long do you think he'll be in there?"

"Not long," Ben said. "He's coming out now."

Eden looked around. Lucas was indeed coming. He hesitated when he saw her waiting, but then he began walking toward them.

"I want to talk to him alone, Ben," she said, watching Lucas approach. His face was as grim as she felt.

"Eden—"

"I promise not to try to beat anything out of him," she said, glancing at him and trying to smile, because she didn't want him to worry. She loved him, too, even if she hadn't said it just now. But she had to do this. She had to know.

He smiled in return. "I'll be right over here," he said.

She watched him walk away. When she looked back, Lucas was standing almost in front of her. She didn't know what he expected from her—more ranting and raving, she supposed. And she had fully intended to give him just that.

But the fight went out of her suddenly, and she stood there staring at him, silent and afraid.

He waited, and she said the only thing in her mind.

"Please…help me."

He gave a sharp exhalation of breath, and she thought he would walk away.

"You don't know what you're asking," he said.

"I'm asking for the truth."

"You're asking for the confused musings of an old man, Ms. Trevoy."

She looked up at him. "Easy for you to say. You know your born-to and born-for clans."

Lucas stood with his arms folded over his chest. Out of the corner of her eye, she could see Ben standing impatiently.

"I *know* he told you something," she said quietly. "And I know it was about me—"

"He told me the name," Lucas interrupted.

"What name?"

"The name of the man he thinks is your father."

"What is it? Tell me."

"I don't have to tell you, Ms. Trevoy. You heard him say it." With that, he walked away, leaving her standing.

"Wait. No—I didn't hear—"

She abruptly stopped and stared after him. The name. She had heard the name.

Lucas Singer.

Chapter Twelve

"Is she still out at your place?"

Toomey glanced up from his paperwork. There was no one else around, and it was the first time he had seen Lucas out of his office in days.

"She doesn't want anything to do with you," Toomey said.

"That's not the question," Lucas said. "The question was, 'Is she still out at your place?'"

"No. She isn't."

"She's in Albuquerque?"

"I don't know. She left the morning after the two of you went to see Billy George. I haven't talked to her since."

"Why not?"

"There's no point in it. This is where I belong, and she doesn't want to come back here—ever."

"She said that?"

"Yes. She said that."

"And that's just fine with you."

"No, it's not just fine with me! But I care enough about her to try to give her what she says she needs. You think it's easy staying away from her? You're just not getting it, sir. Ever since she was a little girl, Eden has put up this wall around herself to keep from being hurt. And the only thing she's learned since Dr. Trevoy died is that that wall wasn't nearly high enough. You know she didn't cry when she found out you were her old man. She didn't say much of anything. I think it hurt too much. You raised three children that weren't yours—but you wouldn't have a damn thing to do with the one that was. Kind of sends her a message, don't you think?"

"I didn't know about her, Toomey. I want you to tell her that."

"It won't do any good. She doesn't want to deal with it. That's why she left and that's why she's not coming back. I'm not going to do anything that will make it worse for her."

"You let it go too long and she'll convince herself leaving was the right thing to do."

"Sir—with all due respect—you're the one who wanted us apart in the first place—"

He stopped because Captain Becenti stood in the doorway.

"Okay, Lucas, let's go," Becenti said. "You, too, Toomey."

"Sir?"

"It's unofficial, Toomey. Don't look so worried."

"I've already had my turn with 'unofficial,' sir. I'm not crazy about doing it again."

"This doesn't have anything to do with the job. It's more a family thing," Becenti said.

"Whose family?" Toomey said.

"Yours, if you play your cards right."

Eden picked up her telephone on the first buzz.

"He's still here waiting," the receptionist said. "And he's very insistent, Ms. Trevoy. He says it's really important."

"What did you say the name was again?"

"A Mr. William Baron."

"Can somebody else help him?"

"He says he was told to ask for you and no one else. Should I tell him you're too busy?"

Eden rubbed the spot between her eyes that hurt.

"No," she said. "I guess not."

"Do you want me to send him to your office?"

"No, I'll come there—and if he's selling insurance, you're in big trouble."

The receptionist laughed, and Eden hung up the phone. She walked down the open staircase into the glass lobby and atrium, looking for this William Baron person as she went. She didn't see anyone she recognized.

"Where is he?" she asked the receptionist.

"Right over there—near the elevators."

She looked at the young man in blue jeans who stood waiting, and she still didn't recognize him. But he apparently knew her. He was already walking in her direction, and when he reached her, he immediately extended his hand.

"William Baron," he said, with a slight but self-assured smile.

"Eden Trevoy," she answered, and his smile broadened.

"I know. Well, I guess you're wondering why I'm here."

"I don't have a lot of time, Mr. Baron."

"Okay, the short version. I'm here, Ms. Trevoy, because—after careful consideration by any number of interested parties—it was decided that I was the messenger of choice."

"Messenger?" she asked, completely baffled. "What kind of messenger? I don't understand."

"The personal kind. I've brought you something."

"What is it?"

"I've brought you a photograph of your mother."

She stared at him.

"Who *are* you?"

"I'm the half-Navajo kid Lucas raised when he should have been raising you. Please—don't look like that. You only know some of the details—but it's the ones you don't know that're causing all the trouble. I'm here to offer you the opportunity to find out what they are—and to help a lot of people—including yourself—in the process."

"This is crazy—"

"Yes. It is. But life seems to be like that."

"*You* are crazy, Mr. Baron," she said, and he laughed.

"Probably so. But you know how it is. When the family needs help, you help."

"No, I don't know how it is. I never had family."

He looked at her for a moment before he continued. She had to glance away from the compassion she saw in his eyes.

"Lucas didn't know about you. Your mother was—"

"I don't want to talk about this. Do you understand?"

"Yes, I understand. And I know how much it annoys you to have somebody say that. I understand that you can't let down your guard and you've got to be really tough. I understand that you can't let anybody tell you what to do or push you around. Live free or die, right? What else can you do when you don't know who you are or where you belong—or what you're going to do about it—''

''Goodbye, Mr. Baron,'' she said, attempting to walk away.

He handed her the photograph, pressing it into her hand before she could refuse to take it. ''Lucas says he'll wait outside for you. He'll tell you what he knows about her, and then, if you want—''

''Look, I told you—''

''I know what you told me, Eden, but you think about it. We'll wait for you outside as long as we can. A lot of people are trying to help you here.''

She shook her head and began to walk away again, the photograph clutched in her hand.

''Eden!'' he called across the lobby. ''One more thing! I want to be the first to say it.''

He waited until she looked back at him, clearly certain that she would.

''Welcome to the family,'' he said.

She didn't look at the photograph until she was safely back in her office. It was the same one that had been in Ben's desk, the one Lucas Singer put into his shirt pocket. She sat there, staring at the smiling young woman who had caused all this turmoil in so many lives.

Lucas didn't know about you.

She didn't believe that he didn't know. Why else would he have been so determined to keep her away from Ben? Lucas hadn't wanted her in his life, even on the fringes of it. Her relationship with a tribal police officer obviously brought her much too close for his personal comfort.

She stayed busy the rest of the afternoon. Or tried to. On the surface she appeared to be functioning, but the only thing she could think about was Lucas Singer waiting outside for her to come talk to him.

She didn't want to talk. She wanted to run as fast and as far as she could.

Lucas didn't know— Yes, he did!

She stayed late, still pretending to earn her salary, and when she finally left the building, she went out through a side entrance, all but running the distance to the parking area and her car. She didn't see anyone around, and she was both disappointed and relieved.

She felt better by the time she reached home, perhaps not quite so torn. She would just have to go back to being the old Eden Trevoy. She could do that, and no one would ever know the real truth. Lucas had said so himself.

I would know, she thought as she walked up the terracotta steps to the front door of the expensive town house that had never felt like home. I would wake up every morning, and I would know I was living a lie. I'm not Eden Trevoy anymore. I'm not—anything.

She unlocked the front door quickly and let herself in, as if she was afraid that Lucas or his messenger might be lurking in the courtyard and might accost her again.

The red light on her answering machine was blinking. She hesitated, then pushed the Play button. She recognized the voice immediately—an old sorority sister with an invitation for drinks and dinner, the one whose brother had assaulted a drunken Indian in the park and who probably wouldn't have gone to jail for it. Eden didn't call her back, because she didn't want to go and because she didn't want the monumental task of trying to think up an excuse for a person who never took no for an answer, anyway. She gave a short laugh. Maybe she should call and just tell her the truth.

I can't go because I'm too busy trying to hide from my Navajo father.

She changed her clothes. She turned on the television and immediately turned it off again. She sat down. She got up and paced around the ground floor. Then she went up to the second floor, to the balcony off the bedroom, and she sat down there and closed her eyes. There was a light and altogether pleasant evening breeze. She could hear the fountain in the courtyard below. She could hear her neighbor, Sugar, the retired lounge singer, playing her baby grand piano.

And she could hear Mrs. Armistead, her elderly neighbor directly across the way, calling her.

"Eden? Eden!"

"Yes, Mrs. Armistead?" Eden called back without getting up.

"Somebody's at your door!"

Eden sighed. "Thank you, Mrs. Armistead!"

"Don't leave, she's coming!" Mrs. Armistead called down to whoever it was.

Eden went downstairs, expecting to find that the invitation for drinks and dinner had come in person.

But Ben Toomey stood on the doorstep. She immediately flung open the door, thinking only at the last second that he might have brought Lucas Singer with him. But alone or not, she was so glad to see him; it was all she could do not to fling herself at him. She had missed him so much!

He was obviously not sure of his welcome. He gave a slight smile and a shrug. "I thought—if you talked to Lucas today—you might need me." He glanced over his shoulder toward where Mrs. Armistead watched from her balcony. "And...I thought—if you *didn't* talk to Lucas today—you might need me."

"Ben—" she said, reaching for him and hugging him tightly in spite of the audience. She did need him. And until now she hadn't realized how much.

"Are you okay?" he asked, leaning back so he could see her face.

"Of course," she said, willing it to be true. "Come inside—can you stay?"

"Do you want me to?"

"Yes, I want you to."

He smiled genuinely this time, the smile she loved. The Ben-Toomey-is-infinitely-pleased one.

She brought him inside, chatting brightly all the while, trying to keep up the pretense that she was just fine. She asked him about Sadie and his mother and Faye. She offered him something to eat and drink. She took him on a tour of the house.

On the way to the balcony, he caught her by both shoulders and made her look at him. "You're not okay, are you? Are you?" he asked again when she didn't answer.

"Not…very," she said, her mouth trembling in spite of all she could do. She leaned against him, and his arms went around her.

"We need to talk," he said, and she nodded, fully intending to do that. And she was only going to give him one small kiss. One. Because she loved him, and because they had been apart too long. But at the first touch of her lips against his, any attempt at conversation immediately fell by the way. He was everything to her, and he was here. She pressed her body against his, letting the wave of longing rush over her. They came together quickly, urgently, without words, both of them driven and needy, both of them trying not to think about all the reasons why they couldn't be together.

"Eden," he said, his eyes staring into hers.

Her body rose to meet his.

"Tell me," he whispered against her ear. "Tell me—"

"I love you, Ben!"

Sugar was playing the piano again. Or perhaps still. Her rich contralto voice drifted up from the courtyard below, her Nina Simone-like rendition of "Black is the Color of My True Love's Hair." It was beautiful, filled with all the yearning and the hunger that Eden herself felt for Ben Toomey. She lay in his arms, quiet now, sated, knowing that she was completely in love with this man and that she was making him miserable.

Her hand lay lightly on his chest.

He put his hand on hers. "When did you know?" he asked.

"Know?"

"That you...had feelings."

She lifted her head to look at him. "Feelings," she repeated, trying not to smile. He was so cute when he was fishing, and she couldn't help but tease him.

"You know what I mean."

"Ah," she said. "Feelings. Let's see. It was the... arroyo."

"I'm serious," he said. "When?"

"I'm serious, too. It was the arroyo. And I can prove it."

He was smiling now. "Yeah? How?"

"When I photographed the 'sun snake' phenomenon, I also photographed Officer Ben Toomey."

"You did not."

"I did, too. A whole bunch of them."

"Yeah?"

"Yeah."

"So...why did you do that?" he said, still fishing.

"You don't want to know," she said.

"Yes, I do," he assured her, hugging her tightly.

"You'll think I'm a loose woman."

"I like loose women," he assured her further, kissing her soundly, the laughter bubbling from her mouth into his.

He was looking into her eyes, and the laughter suddenly faded.

"I love you so much," he said, gravely serious now. "You know that, don't you?"

"Yes," she said. "I know."

"Being with you—making love with you—like this—is wonderful. You're so beautiful, and when I look at you, I can't believe how lucky I am. But I want…more, Eden, and you need to know that, too. I want us to have a life together. You and me and all our children. I want to live with you and grow old with you. I want a marriage like that old couple who owned the trailer had—the 'till death do us part' kind. I don't want us to just take whatever we can get, whenever we can get it. I know how different we are. I know our chances of making it are practically zero, but I still want to try. If you love me enough to want to try, too, well, there's something you're going to have to do first. You're going to have to do it for us and for yourself."

"What?" she asked.

"You're going to have to settle this thing with Lucas Singer. Now."

"Ben—" She tried to move away, but he held on to her.

"There are too many people hurting here, Eden. You're a good person. There's no way you can just ignore that. I know you think, if I loved you, I wouldn't ask you to do something that's so hard for you. I do love you—with all my heart—and I do ask. You need to see him. You need to listen to whatever he has to say. Believing him or not believing him is up to you, but you need to listen. It's the only way—for you and for us. I want us to go to Window Rock tomorrow.''

"Ben, I don't think I can—"

"I'll be with you. You don't have to do it alone.''

"Ben—"

"Tomorrow, Eden. It's the only way.''

He didn't say anything more about it, letting her struggle with her own demons in her own way. She slept fitfully, woke early. She left him sleeping and went out to sit on the balcony. The courtyard was quiet. The sun was about to come up. She watched the gray horizon turn pink, wondering if Lucas Singer faced the eastern sky and chanted to begin each day the way Sadie Benally did.

Red sky at morning, sailor take warning—

The sky wasn't red, and she was about to venture into the desert—but with the foreboding of any seaman who knew he was about to sail into unknown waters on an ill-charted course.

She took a shower and was downstairs making coffee when Ben finally woke. He still made no mention of what he had asked her to do. She wondered if it was part of his Navajo teaching to so eloquently make his case and then to let it go.

They had breakfast together, one seasoned with conversation and laughter. She was amazed at how much they found to talk about besides Lucas Singer. She got up from the table at one point and went to get the photographs she had taken of him in the arroyo.

"Some cop I am—I didn't even have a clue,'' he said, looking through them and chuckling. "I can't believe you did this!''

She smiled sadly. Perhaps she had known even then that whatever happened between her and Ben Toomey, it would end up like her mother's relationship with Lucas Singer—a forgotten photograph in a drawer.

"I have another one I want to show you," she said. She found her purse and gave him the snapshot of the woman who was supposed to be her mother.

"Did you...know who she was?"

"Not until yesterday," he said, looking at it closely. "She does look like you. I didn't realize it before."

She gave a quiet sigh and sat down on his lap, resting her head on his shoulder and bringing her feet up as if she were trying to hide. She wanted to hide. In him. He held her tightly, gently kissing her forehead, but he still didn't badger her.

She closed her eyes for a moment and finally made up her mind.

"Okay," she said. "I'll go."

Chapter Thirteen

They took her car. Ben declined her offer to let him drive. She was going to have to be responsible for all phases of this ordeal herself. It took forever to get to Window Rock—and they still arrived before she was ready.

"Lucas doesn't know I'm coming, does he?" she asked, panicked suddenly by the thought that Ben might have called him and told him, when she was getting dressed. She still needed to know that she could change her mind without anyone—Lucas—being the wiser.

"No," Ben said. "We need to go to his house. If he's off today, he'll be there. If he's working, he'll want to come there to talk to you."

She nodded, but it was all she could do to drive on. She had to force herself to turn where Ben said to turn and to keep on going. Her anxiety doubled when she finally pulled in front of the house where Lucas Singer lived.

"Stop right here," he said, and he turned to face her. "It's going to be all right."

"No, it isn't."

"Yes, it is. It's all downhill from here."

"Easy for you to say, Toomey," she said, and he laughed.

"I really am proud of you, you know that?"

She looked at him doubtfully. "Don't be proud yet."

"You are the strongest and the bravest and the most wonderful woman I've ever known."

"And you're still full of it," she assured him.

He laughed and took her cold hand in his. "Ready?"

"No. But I think I can at least get out of the car."

"Good girl," he said. "Let's go."

They walked hand in hand toward the house.

"Is he here, do you think?" she asked.

"Well, the police car is here—but his truck isn't. Why don't you wait over there?" he said, pointing to a patio area with a picnic table and some wrought iron chairs. "Let me be your go-between. If he's not here, it's probably better if I talk to Sloan."

She looked at him. Sloan. Lucas's wife. Eden hadn't given one single thought to what Sloan must be feeling. Just what the woman needed—to start the day with her husband's long-lost bastard child on her doorstep.

Eden walked over to the patio and sat down in one of the chairs facing a formation of red rock monoliths. The breeze stirred the wind chimes into a delicate tinkling. It was very pleasant here, she thought—except for the circumstances.

After a moment the back door opened and Ben went inside. He didn't stay long, coming out again almost immediately—with Sloan. He gave Eden a small wave and walked back toward the car with no indication as to whether or not she should follow. She stood up, anyway, because Sloan was walking toward her.

"I'm glad you're here," Sloan said without prelude. "Sit down—please—and don't look so worried. Lucas has gone to the men's shelter. My niece—his niece by marriage—and her husband run it. Their phone is out. Ben has gone to tell him you've come. Would you like some coffee?"

"No, thank you," Eden said. And then, "Yes. I think I would."

"Sit down," Sloan said again. "I'll be right back."

She returned with the coffee—and one slice of what looked like cherry pie.

"I thought we'd share this last piece," she said of the pie. "It's my grandmother's recipe. When I was a little girl, she would always tell me that this pie would fix anything that ails me. I think we both need a little fixing today, don't you?"

Eden didn't say anything. She didn't quite know what to do with all this...candor. She took the coffee and half the pie Sloan offered her out of politeness, nibbling at a forkful and finding it quite delicious.

"See?" Sloan said, when Eden took another, bigger bite.

They sat for a time in silence.

"I guess this is really...difficult for you," Eden ventured.

"Yes and no," Sloan said. "Not as difficult as it is for you and Lucas, I think."

"Ben says Lucas didn't know about me."

"He didn't."

"Is that what he told you?"

"No, that's what I know. When I first came out

here—when I first met Lucas, he was still trying to get over his love affair with your mother.''

''I didn't think it was that—a 'love' affair.''

''His hurt and his sense of betrayal was too great for it to have been anything else. And it was a big obstacle in my deciding whether or not I would take a chance and marry him—aside from the cultural differences and all that.''

''But it's worked out—your marriage,'' Eden said. ''Even with all the differences?''

''Well, so far so good, as they say. But it isn't always easy—for either of us.''

''Then why do you stay married?''

Sloan laughed softly. ''Because of the love we have for each other. And because, from the first, we agreed to hang in there—no matter what.''

''Did you know her—the…woman in the photograph?'' Eden asked, struggling to find some way to identify the person who had given birth to her without using the word ''mother.'' ''Or did you even see the photograph?''

''Yes, I saw it. But I didn't know her, not really. I met her once—no, twice,'' Sloan said.

''What was she like?''

''Beautiful face. Expensive clothes. Wealthy family. Very focused.''

''Focused?''

''On what she wanted.''

''You didn't like her.''

''I didn't know her. I only knew the pain she caused.''

They stared at each other across the table.

''Do you know where she is now?'' Eden asked.

Sloan looked at her for a moment, but she was saved from having to answer by the sound of a car. ''Ben is back,'' she said. ''I'm going into the house. I think you and Lucas need to talk alone.'' She began to walk away, but then she stopped and turned around. "Eden—thank you—for coming today. It's the right thing to do, and I'm more grateful than you'll ever know.''

Lucas pulled into the drive. Eden took a deep breath as he got out of the truck and walked in their direction. He said something to Sloan that Eden couldn't hear. Sloan answered him, but when she would have walked on by, Lucas caught her hand for a moment and held it to his chest. He didn't say a word, but there were so many things in that one small gesture—love and respect, admiration and gratitude and trust.

"Are you still up for this?" Ben said at her elbow.

"Yes," Eden said, still watching.

"I'm going to go into the house while you and Lucas talk, but I'll be close."

She nodded, finally looking at him. He was so worried about her, and not without good reason. It was all she could do not to bolt.

"I'm okay," she said with an assurance she didn't begin to feel. "I can do this."

He smiled and reached up to lightly caress her cheek. Then he left her there. It was all she could do not to run after him and tell him to get her away from here. She kept glancing at Lucas as he approached. She had no sense of what he must be thinking or feeling at all. And she couldn't even begin to guess.

He didn't say anything when he reached the patio, and neither did she. She stood looking at the monoliths.

"I...didn't think you'd come," he said finally.

"Neither did I," she answered. "You know," she said, suddenly turning to him. "This could all be for nothing. You said it yourself. It could all be the ramblings of a confused old man—"

"It's not."

"How do you know?"

"I know because I talked to your mother day before yesterday."

"That...must have been an interesting conversation."

He didn't say anything, and when she finally looked at him, he was trying not to smile.

"What?" she asked pointedly. She failed to see any humor in this situation.

The smile broadened, then faded away. "Nothing. I was just wondering where you got that razor-sharp wit of yours. I'm glad you have it. I expect you've needed it."

"It comes in handy when people try to intimidate me."

"Yes, I've noticed."

"So what did my...mother say? Did she deny ever having a baby girl?"

"Yes," he answered. "She did."

She looked at him, a bit taken aback by how much that answer hurt.

"So we're back to square one."

"No. Her husband told me the truth."

"Why would he do that?"

"Because he was ashamed. All these years—since we were roommates in college—I thought he was my friend. I believed him when he told me she had gotten rid of my child. He told me she had had an abortion—because he knew me well enough—they both knew me well enough—to know that that was the only thing that could keep me from trying to find you."

"If *she* didn't want me, why would she care if you did?"

"She didn't want her family to find out about it. If I had you, she thought there was a chance that they might. Somebody might see you, somebody who knew about her and me, who would guess where I got you. Apparently her family and their social circle frowns on illegitimate, half-breed children. She would have lost her trust fund.''

"And she ended up marrying *your* friend, the liar.''

"Yes.''

"So what was this lovely person's name?''

"Her name was Sara Catherine McCay. Sara Catherine Wager now.''

"She lives around here?''

"She lives near Santa Fe—although I did get the impression that that was about to change.''

"Why? Does she think I'm going to bother her, try to see her?''

"She specifically asked that I not bring you there.''

"I don't need or want anything from her. I guess she must not know that my trust fund is probably a lot bigger than hers,'' she said sarcastically.

She looked past him. She could see Ben's face briefly in the kitchen window.

"Do you still love her?'' she asked bluntly, and Lucas laughed.

"I still...remember her. I was too stupid and inexperienced to see what was happening at the time. I didn't understand the situation at all. I was too busy being flattered that someone like her would want to be with someone like me. I didn't know that there were people who use other people for their own amusement—people who lie when they don't have to. Love isn't the word for what she and I had.''

She walked away a few steps.

"But that doesn't mean I wouldn't have loved you—if I'd had the chance,'' he said.

"It's a moot point now, Lieutenant. But—at least I can

understand why you were so worried about Ben. Why you're *still* so worried."

He made no attempt to deny it. She hadn't been raised *by* Sara Catherine McCay, but she'd been raised *like* her. Eden couldn't deny that. Even without knowing who she was, Lucas had looked at her and seen another rich girl on the prowl.

The silence lengthened. She stood looking at the red rocks again.

"Your mother and I hurt you a great deal," Lucas said. "And for that I—"

"It doesn't matter," she interrupted, because she thought he was about to say he was sorry, and she didn't want him to do it. He had been her adversary from the first time she'd met him. She didn't want to change that. She didn't want to feel empathy or anything else where he was concerned. It was so much safer not to feel. "I don't need anything from you, either, Lieutenant. I'm way past needing a father at this late date."

He looked surprised—and hurt—by the remark. Surely he didn't think that they could have some kind of parent-child relationship now. She was a grown woman. She had needed him when she was five and afraid of the dark. She had needed him when she was sent away to boarding school. Where was he then?

"Yes," he said. "I suppose you are. If you have any more questions—if there's anything else you want to know—"

"No," she said. "No more questions. It—"

"—doesn't matter," he finished for her. "I understand. I would like to ask you to do one thing, though."

"What is it?" she said, her attention wandering because Ben had just stepped out of the house.

"I want you to wait here just a little longer," Lucas said.

"Why?"

"For the sake of your family."

"I don't have a family," she said, looking back at him.

But even as she said it, two cars pulled into the driveway.

"I'm afraid you do," Lucas said. "Your grandmother wants to see you."

"My...grandmother?"

"She's an old woman, Eden. She was with me when Ben came to tell me you were here. I couldn't say no to her. You don't have to speak to her if you don't want to. Just let her see you."

"Lieutenant—"

"She's done a lot of crying since she heard about you. I'm asking you for her sake, not mine."

Eden could see the elderly woman getting out of the car. She was having difficulty walking, and a young man was helping her—William Baron, who had come to the bank and who had been the first to welcome Eden Trevoy to the Singer family.

Ben walked up, and Eden reached out to take his hand, in a panic now as more people approached—two men and two women—three small children. One of the women had flaming red hair.

"I don't want to do this," she whispered to Ben.

"Okay," he said. "Then we'll go."

She looked up at him. He meant it. He had asked her to come here, but he wouldn't try to make her stay. Somehow, that was all she needed to know.

The old woman—her grandmother—had reached the edge of the patio. Two of the children—a little girl, obviously red-haired like her mother—and a dark-haired boy—scurried ahead of her and placed a red-and-black pillow carefully in the nearest chair. The old woman's progress was slow at best, but with William Baron's help, she was finally able to sit down.

Eden took a deep breath. "No—I—it's okay," she said, but she didn't let go of Ben's hand. She suddenly recognized that the dark-haired woman approaching was the lawyer, Lillian Becenti. No—Lillian *Singer*-Becenti.

"Eden," Lillian said. "What a surprise this is." She stepped forward with a little boy in her arms and kissed Eden's cheek. "Just so you can get this all straight—besides being your favorite lawyer—I'm also your aunt—and this one here," she said of the boy, "is your cousin, Charlie. And this is my husband—Captain Johnny Becenti of the Navajo Tribal Police. You know how it is with us Singer women," she said to Ben. "Navajo tribal police officers are *it* for us. I think it must be the uniform."

"Got to be that," Ben said.

"The first time we met, I knew you reminded me of somebody," she whispered to Eden. "*Me*. We don't take any crap off anybody, do we, baby?"

The little boy—Charlie—reached out and grabbed Eden by her jacket front, and she had no alternative but to take him. He threw one small arm around her neck and grinned, determined to participate in whatever this turned out to be.

"As you can see," Lillian told her, "he takes after his mother. He's *very* shy."

Eden couldn't help but laugh, and Charlie laughed with her, nose crinkled, fist against his mouth, as if he had understood the joke perfectly.

"I'm Meg," the young red-haired woman said. "Lucas is my uncle by marriage, Sloan is my aunt. I'm your...well, we'll figure that out later. This is my husband, Jack," she said of the Navajo man with her. "Our children, Tad and Julia. You won't meet my older brother Patrick today—he's in Flagstaff working. But you already know my younger brother Will.''

William Baron, who was still stationed by the old woman's chair, gave Eden a little wave.

"I'm the hell-raiser of the family," Meg's husband, Jack, whispered, shaking her hand. "So don't worry. If Lucas let *me* in, the door is wide open for you."

There was no one left for Eden to be introduced to now but her grandmother. The old woman sat in her chair, leaning forward expectantly, her hands clutching the arms of the chair. Lillian took her son back, and Eden stood there, not knowing quite what to do.

"I don't know her name," she whispered to Ben.

"Dolly," Ben said. "Your grandmother's name is Dolly."

"Singer?"

"Yes."

Dolly said something and motioned for Eden to come closer.

"She can't see very well, Eden," Will said. "You need to be close."

Eden hesitated a moment, then walked forward. But Dolly still had difficulty seeing her, and Eden finally knelt down by her chair. Dolly immediately began to speak to her in Navajo.

"She says she is still breathless from getting here so quick," Will translated. "She was afraid you would leave before she got here. She is glad you came and she is very grateful to Ben for bringing you home. She wants to know if it would offend you if she touched you."

"No," Eden said. "It wouldn't offend me."

The old woman reached up to lightly stroke Eden's hair, then immediately asked a question.

"She wants to know what happened to your hair," Will said. "She thinks it's very...um, short."

Eden gave Ben a pointed look, and he laughed and immediately began to give what she hoped was an explanation of the hair situation.

"Ben told her his sister Faye got hold of you," Will said. "Dolly thinks somebody better start hiding the scissors from this girl."

Dolly smiled and began to speak again. She reached up with both hands to lightly explore Eden's face with her fingertips.

"She says she can tell that you are very beautiful—but she can feel that you've lost your *hozro*. She says your harmony is gone and you must try to get it back now—and not be so angry—"

"I'm not angry—" Eden said, but Dolly took both her hands and held them gently between hers. Eden could feel how fragile they were—and how strong, all at the same time.

"She says when you were a child, it was right for you to be angry with Lucas—he was your father and he wasn't there when you needed him. You couldn't know then that that wasn't what he wanted. But the woman you are now can see the truth.

"Dolly says you waste your anger on Lucas and on the white woman who refused to be your mother. And you waste your anger on the one who died. *She* did wrong to take you away from the People—but she didn't do wrong in giving you the chance to live. That woman gave you life as surely as the ones you were born to and born for, and you need to remember that, instead of the things she did that were bad for you.

"Dolly says that she is so sorry she missed the time when you were a little girl—it makes her very sad—be-

cause there are many things about Mother Earth and Father
Sky she would have liked to have shown you. It's too late
now, she says. You're not a little girl anymore, and her
eyes are too dim. That beauty time, that little-girl time, has
rushed away and vanished—like a cloud before the wind.
It won't ever come back again. But she wants you to know
that before you were real to us, when you were like a
faraway star, even then she loved you—''

Will suddenly stopped. ''You okay, Eden?'' he asked
quietly.

She bit down on her lower lip to keep her mouth from
trembling. Her eyes burned and her throat ached. It was
all she could do not to cry. But she stayed by Dolly's chair,
her head bowed, struggling for control. It was only with
the greatest effort that she was able to look up at Dolly
again.

''Yes,'' she said, her voice barely audible. ''I'm sorry.
I didn't mean to—'' She took a deep breath. ''Please, go
on,'' she said to her grandmother. ''I'm listening.''

''Dolly says she knows she will love the woman you
have become,'' Will continued. ''And she wants you to let
your heart be at ease now. She says your father is a good
man and Ben is a good man. She says they can help you
when you don't understand the ways of the People. She
says she wants you to remember that you aren't alone anymore—and she asks when Ben will marry you,'' he con-
cluded.

''What?'' Eden said, startled.

''She says she hopes you won't wait too long to have a
wedding with him, because she is getting old, and she
doesn't want to miss that, too.''

Will offered Eden his hand, and she stood up. Dolly
continued to talk, but she was speaking to Ben now, who

came and knelt down on one knee, so that he wouldn't tower over her.

"What are they saying?" Eden asked Will.

"Well—as the head of the family, she's kind of asking him if his intentions toward you are honorable."

"Are they?"

"Damn straight," Will said. "You've got too many warriors in your family for him to trifle with your affections. We kick butt first and ask questions later."

She smiled at his teasing, in spite of how close she'd been to tears.

After a moment Ben stood up.

"Dolly says the two of you should go now," Will said. "She says her granddaughter's heart is sad and she needs some time to find her harmony again. She says Ben should take you to a quiet place, because you have much to think about. She says you have a home here now, and all of us will be waiting for you to return."

Home, Eden thought.

The concept was still foreign to her. These people had been very gracious and accepting. But there was nothing she wanted to say to them, nothing she *could* say. Even the idea of really having a family—for her—bordered on the bizarre. The actuality was absolutely overwhelming. A token goodbye to them was the most she could manage, one not addressed to anyone in particular, one with no promise of doing this again sometime.

She looked around, expecting Lucas to be standing near the edge of the patio, but he was no longer there.

"He walked down to the corral, Eden," Will said. "He's...upset. He didn't want you to see it."

Eden stood for a moment, then walked off in that direction, leaving everyone else behind. She saw Lucas immediately. He was saddling one of the horses.

"I'm going now," she said, and if he made any kind of reply, she didn't hear it.

"Look," she said. "I don't know what you expected—"

"I didn't expect anything," he said. "It's enough that you came."

She stood there, not knowing what to say. "It's too late," she said finally. "Can't you see that?"

He didn't answer her.

"I don't know if I can do what Dolly says. I don't know if I can let go of the anger. I don't know how to be—whatever it is I am—half Sara Catherine McCay and half you. I don't know what to do with the love and the kindness all of you are trying to give me. I just don't know!"

"I understand," he said. He went back to saddling the horse.

But she didn't want him to understand. She didn't want anything—except perhaps...her father.

She began to walk away.

"Eden—" Lucas called after her.

She looked back at him.

"There is something I expect," he said. "I expect you to have a good and happy life. You tell Ben Toomey he had better take care of my daughter."

It was the last thing she expected him to say, and she almost smiled. She stood for a moment, then smiled after all.

"I'll tell him," she said.

Ben waited for her at the end of the driveway, and she looked at him gratefully when he put his hand on her shoulder to walk back to the car.

The love of my life, she thought. *Ben—*

"So how's it going?" he asked quietly.

"Okay," she said, but she was close to crying again.

"You're not mad at me, are you? For asking you to do this?"

"No," she said. He had been right about her talking to Lucas. Whether it accomplished anything or not, it needed to be done.

"You know you're more or less engaged now, don't you?" Ben said as they walked along.

"Am I?" she said, leaning against him, needing his warmth and his strength.

"Oh, yes. I've declared my intentions to the undisputed, matriarchal head of your family. Offered horses for you and everything. It's practically a done deal."

"Oh, well, then. If it's a done deal," she said. "How many horses?"

"A lot," he said. "A *whole* lot."

"That many," she said, trying to hold up her end of the banter. "What else will you give for me?"

"Anything."

"Anything?"

"Anything," he insisted.

She dared to ask the question. "Time?"

"As much as you need."

"You'll wait—until I get used to all this? Until I can—?" She stopped. She didn't know what her ultimate goal was—except to be worth all the horses he supposedly offered for her.

He stopped walking and put both arms around her.

"I love you, Eden," he said. "However long it takes, I'll wait."

"I'm scared, Ben!" she said, clinging to him. "What if we can't make it?"

"We're not going to worry about the what-ifs. It's not going to be easy—but nothing worth having ever is."

She leaned back to look at him. "I told Harrison you were the love of my life," she said.

He smiled broadly. "And stunted his growth, probably."

"You *are* the love of my life—but I still have to—" She stopped before she cried.

He held her tightly. "I love you," he said again. "I'll keep the horses ready. I'll wait."

Chapter Fourteen

He made it through the metal detector.

"Joey's going to be thrilled," Eden said, surprising him because she remembered what he had told her about Joey Nez wanting to challenge the airport metal detector, and because she could actually attempt a joke—albeit mild.

He himself was totally miserable. She was leaving—for who knew how long. He hadn't slept. He didn't feel like eating. And he was supposed to sit here with her and then watch her get on a plane, pretending all the while that it was all right with him that she was going. It wasn't all right. He didn't care what he had told her the day she'd gone to talk to Lucas Singer. It was *not* all right.

"This is really a good career move," he said abruptly. "It'll look good on your résumé."

"Yes," she said. "They don't usually send someone as newly hired as I am off to do the New York thing."

"And it came at a good time," he suggested, knowing

he was about to walk right off the end of the pier here. He was going to keep at it until he told her exactly how he felt about her leaving. And then she'd think he hadn't meant what he said about giving her time. And then she'd go off to New York mad, and he'd have his feelings all hurt and he'd probably go looking for trouble somewhere and find it—and then he'd feel a whole lot worse than he already did.

Just shut up! he admonished himself.

He tried looking out the window. There wasn't much to see but the baggage handlers and an occasional flight taxiing in.

"Ben, you'll call me?" she asked, looking at him in that way she had that made his knees weak and made him want to—

Oh, Eden—

"As often as you can," she said, taking his hand. "I don't care what time it is—if you get the chance, just call, okay?"

"Okay," he said.

"And I'll call—I'll give Mary Skeets my phone number—as soon as I know what it is—if you're not there."

"Okay," he said again. This was going to work out—because it had to work out. And all he had to do was what he said he'd do. Wait. He could do that—maybe—if he could just quit thinking of this trip as the coup de grâce for an already doomed relationship.

"If you don't stop!" Eden said, giving him a small punch on the arm.

"What?" he asked, startled. "Stop what?"

"Suffering!" she said, making a young couple with two small children turn around and look.

"I would if I could," he assured her.

"I need to do this, Ben—"

"I know that," he said. "I know it's for the best. You've got to be away from here for a while—and away from Lucas—and all the hassle—"

And away from me.

"Then help me," she said.

"Eden, I'm trying to, but this is killing me. I can wait—as long as it takes. But I'm damned if I can be happy about it."

They both sighed.

"It's not that I have to be away from *you*," she said, as if he had voiced that concern. "It's that you're all tangled up with everything else here. And I—"

They were announcing her flight, and she began to gather up her belongings. He walked with her as far as he was allowed to go.

She looked up at him and gave him a half smile. "You know, Toomey, I was hoping for a little more than a handshake and a pat on the head here," she said.

He reached for her then and kissed her as if he would never see her again. Then he abruptly let her go.

"I have to get out of here," he said, and he walked rapidly away without looking back.

Everything is going to be okay.

Everything is not going to be okay!

Find the harmony.

Find it!

But harmony was nothing if not elusive. The harder you chased after it, the more it fled. It was like running after your own shadow. You had to be quiet—mentally, physically and spiritually—and let it come to you. He knew that; he just couldn't do it.

He drove back to Window Rock instead of stopping to see Joey at the medical center—when he more or less said he would. Just what he needed—guilt heaped on top of misery.

His spirits lifted slightly when he drove into the parking lot at the law enforcement building, because it was nearly empty. No catastrophes here at least—or maybe a catastrophe was exactly what he needed to take his mind off his troubles. Big decision—did he want to be busy or did he want to feel sorry for himself?

"Ben!" Mary Skeets called the minute he walked in the door.

He stopped, but he didn't want to.

Mary didn't say anything.

"What!" he said finally, because she was staring at him and she wasn't exactly being forthcoming.

"You look so bad I almost hate to do this."

"Oh, please," he said. "Go ahead. Give me your best shot."

"I think Eden's mother is here."

He held up both hands. "Well, you got me, Mary. Right through the heart." He began to walk away.

"Ben—no, wait. I'm serious. She's here. She asked for Lucas, but he's at a tribal council meeting. I don't know what to do with her. Lucas probably isn't coming back here today and I don't want to send this woman to his *house.* I mean Sloan would be there and everything, and who wants an old flame your husband had a baby with showing up at your door—"

"Mary, is there a point to this somewhere?"

"Yes, Ben, there is. I thought since you and Eden were—together—you could maybe just talk to her and see what she wants."

"I'd rather stick hot needles into my eyes," he said.

"But you'll do it, right? It might be something important—to Eden."

"Mary, I just put Eden on a plane for New York. I don't know how long she's going to be gone. I don't even know if she's coming back. I'm telling you I'm not up for this—"

"But you'll do it, right? If that woman is here to cause trouble, you ought to know about it, right?"

"Mary—"

He just *hated* it when she was this logical.

"Just go talk to her."

"Now, you *know* the minute I do, Lucas is going to come walking through that door—because that's the kind of day I'm having. Then he's going to have a fit and I'm going to catch hell—"

"Are you going to do it or not!"

"Yes!"

"Well, good!"

"So where is she?" he asked grumpily.

"I had her sit down at your desk."

"Great. The royalty treatment. That ought to put her in a good mood."

She was still sitting there, Eden's so-called mother. He noted immediately that she was a very attractive woman—in an artificially youthful sort of way—and that she still looked very much like her daughter, except that nothing about her seemed real—hair, face, nails. He wondered idly what a woman with fingernails like that did all day long.

"Are *you* going to tell me where Lucas Singer is?" she asked him immediately, not giving him a chance to even introduce himself.

Okay, he thought. No amenities.

"No, I'm going to try to find out what you're doing here," he said.

"What I'm doing here is none of your business."

"If nothing else, I'm allowed to be curious," he said. "I'm going to marry your daughter."

That got her attention. She looked at him and smiled.

"Does *she* know that?" she asked, as if she found these delusions of grandeur he was having most amusing.

"Lucas is unavailable," he said, getting back to the topic at hand. "Is there anything I can do for you?"

"Certainly not," she said. "This is personal."

"Okay," he assured her and turned to go.

"I suppose you think you know all the details," she said. "About me."

He looked at her. "I know enough."

"Did you know I tried to get my daughter back?"

The assertion was too incredible for him to bother with.

"Did you?" she asked again.

"No," he answered. "I didn't."

"Dr. Trevoy was a very unforgiving woman. First, she wouldn't let me see my own baby when I wanted to. Sometimes, I just wanted to *see* her, you know? Then, she sent that child—*my* child—off to a private school someplace so I couldn't find her. She said I couldn't keep changing my mind all the time. She said it was too late for me to decide I wanted to play motherhood—because this was a little girl and not a dress on the sale rack—like I didn't know that. Edna Trevoy was very...disagreeable."

"But you kept looking for your daughter, right?"

The question surprised her. "I...would have," she said. "If..." She stopped and looked away.

But he knew "if" what. Eden had told him. It was a very simple equation. One bastard, half-breed kid equaled one lost trust fund. *He* knew the real reason she didn't look, but he wondered if *she* did.

"That's too bad," he said. "Never getting to know Eden is your loss. Believe me."

"Look," she said. "I just need to know what Lucas and...my daughter have decided. That's all."

"About what?"

"About *me*. God, you're dense. I don't want my life disrupted. Surely, you can understand that."

He stood there for a moment, struggling to stay civil. His upbringing required it. His job required it. His love for Eden required it.

"I don't think they've decided anything," he said evenly. "Eden rarely mentions you."

"You might as well know," she said, "I have no intention of financing any little projects she—or you—may have."

"I see," he said, hanging on with his last ounce of self-control. "I was wondering, Mrs...."

"Wager," she said, clearly surprised that he—who was supposed to be marrying her daughter—didn't know it.

"Eden has never mentioned your married name," he said as if she had asked him to explain his ignorance. "I was wondering how you feel about...grandchildren."

"I beg your pardon?"

"Grandchildren—the children of one's child. You know."

"I have no idea what you're talking about."

"Well, actually, I'm talking about me. You see, I intend to give you grandchildren, Mrs. Wager. Many, *many* grandchildren. I suppose I should keep them all on the rez and out of your sight, right? Eden, too, while I'm at it. No loading up the troops and crashing your dinner parties."

"I have a right to my privacy," she said, making a point of leaning forward and reading his name tag.

"Maybe," he said. "Adoption laws keep changing, though. DNA testing keeps improving. Wills get...contested. Are your parents—Eden's grandparents—still living?'' he asked mildly.

She paled visibly. ''I don't find this conversation amusing at all, Mr. Toomey.''

''Officer Toomey. No, I don't imagine you do.''

''All right, what is it you want?''

''Well, since you asked, I want you to take yourself back to wherever you came from. And I want you to stay there, unless and until Eden sends for you. And if she ever does, I want you to try to have a little compassion and don't come at her like you think she's some kind of parasite. This situation isn't about you. It's about her trying to find out who she is and where she belongs. She knows *why* Dr. Trevoy agreed to take her. And even if she did want your money—which she doesn't—everything you have wouldn't be enough to cancel out the grief you've given her. Learning the truth has been really hard for her, but Eden is strong. And she's beautiful and she's smart. And I don't want *you* disrupting *her* life, Mrs. Wager, any more than Miss Edna did. Not now. Not ever.''

She looked at him a long moment. ''There was a time,'' she said quietly, ''when Eden's father would have stood up for me...the way you just did for her. She's a lucky woman. I hope she doesn't screw everything up the way I did.''

She abruptly stood and picked up her purse, and she hesitated as if she wanted to say something more. But then she pushed past him—and Mary Skeets, who just ''happened'' to be standing by the door.

He sat down heavily at his desk, knowing it would only be a matter of seconds before Mary offered her critique.

''Nice going,'' she said almost immediately at his elbow.

He rubbed his eyes and leaned back in the chair.

"But maybe you shouldn't have threatened her," she added.

He looked at her. "Threaten her? I didn't threaten——oh, yeah, I did, didn't I?" he said wearily.

"So," Mary said. "How many grandchildren are you and Eden planning on giving her?"

Catastrophes were better, he decided after his encounter with Mrs. Wager. At least they passed the time. But the truth of the matter was that he didn't know what to do with himself with Eden gone. He followed the same schedule he had always followed regarding work and family, but he was so…lonely. Everything he saw or did, every place he went, his only interest in it was what she would think about it, or how she would laugh, or that she alone would appreciate the subtle irony. And the nights. He could lie in his bed and almost—almost—feel her, smell her, taste her. Whoever said absence makes the heart grow fonder surely had Ben Toomey in mind.

He talked to Eden on the phone—when they could catch up with each other. He was forever out someplace and she was forever "in conference." When they did manage to reach each other, he tried not to sound as if he was suffering.

And, it didn't help that he had that little voice inside his head, the one telling him and telling him that he had better get used to not having her, because this could well be permanent. Who knew when she would come back? Who knew *if* she'd come?

Oddly enough he got the best advice from Lucas Singer.

"If you can't stand it anymore, go get her," Lucas said.

"I said I'd give her time," Toomey told him.

"Toomey," Lucas said. "I told you before. It's easy for

people to get used to the status quo. It's safe and nobody gets hurt. *Go get her.*"

So he dipped into his savings and he went—unannounced—right into one of the most prestigious banking establishments in the world—where he stuck out among all those Wall Street types like the proverbial sore thumb. It was raining. He was wet and cold. Naturally the security people weren't about to let him just walk in off the street like that and see her. Even he would have to admit that he didn't look like somebody associated in any way whatsoever with investment banking, and while he appreciated the fact that Eden was well protected, this whole thing was a nuisance. He insisted that Ms. Trevoy be advised that he was here, and with a flash of his tribal police credentials, a security guard—an extremely suspicious woman with intricately braided hair—and another Mary Skeets if he ever saw one—finally agreed to buzz Ms. Trevoy and give her a message.

"There's a man here to see you," she said. "He says to tell you—are you sure this is right?" she asked Toomey, looking again at what he had scribbled on her memo pad.

"Yes. Tell her that. Word for word."

"He says to tell you he thinks his horses are going to die of old age."

There must have been complete silence on the other end of the line.

Then, "She wants to know if you're cute," the guard whispered to him. "Yeah, *real* cute," she reported to Eden.

"Sexy brown eyes?" the guard said—loud enough for half the lobby to hear. "Just a second. Let me see." She made a point of looking and trying to decide. "You betcha," she said.

"In that case," she reported to Toomey, "Ms. Trevoy will be right down."

"Which direction will she be coming from?"

"She'll get off those elevators right there. You just stand where you are, and she can see you no matter which one she comes down on."

"Thanks," he said, glancing at her and then back again because she was grinning so.

"What?" he said.

"You are *good*, baby, you know that? That thing about the horses you said? I ain't *never* heard a line like that, and believe me, I have heard them *all*. I didn't think she'd go for it—you talking about horses and looking like a wet dog—but you are *good*."

He laughed. "Thanks," he said again. "But she hasn't seen the wet dog part yet."

"She's not going to care about that. You should have heard that girl's voice light up when she knew it was you. You are the *man*."

It took a number of minutes for Eden to get there. It took a lifetime. And the guard was right. She didn't care if he was wet. She leaped into his arms, not caring what the banking community thought. He couldn't kiss her enough, hold her enough.

"I can't believe you're here," she kept saying.

"Where else would I be? I love you—"

And then she looked into his eyes. "Get those horses ready, Toomey—I'm coming home."

Epilogue

Sometimes Toomey thought that Miss Edna had planned for this to happen, that perhaps she had seen something in him when he and Eden were children, some facet of his character or some indicator of his spirit and spunk that made her think that *he* was the one who should accompany her adopted daughter when she made her long journey home. When Miss Edna manipulated his arrival at the arroyo, she had deliberately set the plan in motion, sowing the seeds of possibility, as it were, and perhaps hoping for the best.

Sometimes he leaned more toward Sadie's assessment of the situation—that every now and then the Holy People take pity on human beings and deign to straighten out the messes they've gotten themselves into. Only it was his opinion that this situation wasn't a self-induced mess so much as it was simply wrong. Eden belonged to the People. She had been taken away without her father knowing.

It was only reasonable that she should be brought home again, by whatever convoluted means were necessary.

But in the end, it didn't really matter. He and Eden had three whole days together before he had to return to Window Rock. He told her about Mrs. Wager's visit, and she was quiet for a time, but not as sad as she might have been. It took another whole month to get Eden back to Albuquerque—the spirit was willing but the bank demurred. And nearly five more months before they could be married. In the end she gave up Albuquerque and concentrated her considerable skills on helping the tribe wheel and deal its assets into capital gains.

And now, after a year of being her husband, he had no doubts whatsoever that it was well worth the wait—*she* was well worth the wait—

"Okay, Ben, here we go—lift her up—hold her. Push, Eden! I can see him—push! *Push!* One more time and he's here—*push!*"

"Sloan—I can't—" Eden said, gasping. "I can't—Ben—"

"Yes, you can!" Sloan said. "Do it! Now! Push!"

He braced himself just in time as Eden gave a long cry and one more mighty push and collapsed into his arms.

"All right!" Sloan said. "Look at *this*—a baby *boy*—" She was working rapidly now, doing things Ben couldn't see and then suctioning the baby's mouth and throat.

After a brief moment, the baby began to wail.

"Perfect!" Sloan cried. "It's 8:57 p.m. Happy birthday, sweet thing! Here you go—Eden—Ben—here he is—" She laid him carefully across Eden's belly. "Move your knee a little bit so I can still see him. So what do you think? Is he beautiful or what?"

"Oh," Eden said, taking his tiny hand. "Look at him, Ben—"

He held her tightly, kissed her cheek. And it was all he could do not to bawl right along with his son.

"He's—okay?" he asked Sloan when he thought he could trust his voice, extending a tentative finger to touch his little boy.

"Well, it was a bumpy ride—it's going to take a day or two for him to pretty up. But he is *fine*—and mad," she added as the baby wailed louder. "I know," she said, reaching up to rub the baby on his back. "You were minding your own business and just look what happened—"

Ben couldn't help but smile—because that assessment kind of fit him and Eden, too—their entire courtship and marriage and journey into parenthood—in a nutshell.

"You want to cut the cord?" Sloan asked him.

"I don't know," he said, startled. "Do I?"

"Of course, you do. Let Eden down easy and come around here."

He grinned. "Okay," he said. "You aren't going to let me do something wrong, are you?"

"No, silly. Take these. Cut right there—*right* there. See? Nothing to it. Now pull that stool up and sit down over there next to Eden. Virginia is going to take your boy and tune him up a little bit—over there in the corner— weigh him and print him—then you get to hold him while I finish up here."

He moved the stool and sat down, taking Eden into his arms as much as he could without upsetting whatever Sloan was doing. She was completely exhausted. He stroked her hair, her face.

"Ben?" she said drowsily. "He's so beautiful—"

"Takes after his mother," he said, and she managed a laugh.

"Oh, yeah. I'm just gorgeous—"

"You are," he said, looking into her eyes. And he was very close to bawling again.

The nurse, Virginia, brought his son and placed him carefully into his arms.

"Here you go, Ben," she said. "No, wait. Slide that way a little bit so Eden can see him, too."

"What do I do?" he asked.

"Nothing. Just hold him."

"I can handle that," he said.

He sat there, looking down at his baby's face, rocking him gently and glancing at Eden from time to time. She was right. This boy was beautiful—incredibly beautiful.

His mind went to the women in his family, to his mother and Sadie and Faye, all of whom had been sent for when the baby announced his hasty intent to be born, but who had not yet arrived.

And Dolly Singer.

Someone—Will Baron, he thought—had gone to get her and bring her here. Her precarious health had stabilized of late, as if she had been anticipating this sudden eventuality.

But the baby had come too quickly for any of the family to be in attendance, save his very nervous father, and his stepgrandmother, who had delivered him, and his tribal police lieutenant grandfather, who still paced outside in the hall. It had both surprised and pleased Toomey that Lucas had dropped everything and come along to the hospital with him when the call came that Eden was in labor and the birth imminent.

"Okay," Sloan said finally. "I'm done here. How are you feeling, Eden?"

"Almost as good as Ben does," she murmured, reaching out to touch his arm, and Sloan laughed.

"I expect there are all kinds of born-to and born-for grandmothers and great-grandmothers and aunts ready to pounce on this baby boy and give him his first bath,'' she said. ''But the doctor has to check him first—so let me go and see if he's ready to do that. Ben, you help me hold them off.''

''I'll try,'' he said, knowing the plan was likely hopeless because he could already hear a commotion outside in the hall.

Sloan opened the door, and he and Eden and their baby were immediately caught in a flurry of ancient and modern rituals, with both factions equally determined to be satisfied. The most he could manage was to stay out of the way, and it was only after the Singer-Toomey-Benally womenfolk had departed and Eden was finally sleeping quietly in her room that he realized that one person had been conspicuously absent.

Lucas.

Toomey found him outside the building, staring at the first pink edge of the sunrise.

''Sir?'' he said when he was still some distance away, not wanting to startle him.

''Toomey,'' Lucas said, obviously startled, anyway. ''Everything okay?''

''Yes, sir. Eden's fine—she's asleep. And the baby—'' He stopped, suddenly overwhelmed by the realization that he—Benjamin Toomey—was henceforth and forevermore...a father. He swallowed heavily and took a deep breath.

''You want to see him, sir?'' he asked after a moment.

''You think it would be all right?'' Lucas asked, Toomey thought because Lucas and Eden were still learning how to be father and daughter, and clearly he didn't want to presume.

''I think it would be fine, sir. Eden's going to ask me

what you think of him. And I can't very well say, if you don't come look, can I?''

Lucas actually smiled. "No," he said. "I guess not."

They walked back inside together. The baby was still in the nursery—newly born, newly examined, newly washed by a small legion of female relatives who already loved him. Toomey tapped lightly on the glass to get the nurse's attention, and she immediately came to the door.

"His grandfather would like to hold him," Toomey whispered, taking it upon himself to make the request on Lucas's behalf.

"Oh, sure. Come in, Lieutenant Singer," she said, holding the door wider. "Put on one of those paper gowns there and have a seat in that rocking chair."

Lucas hesitated, but only briefly. He followed the nurse inside and put on the gown while she went to the bassinet.

"Right there," she said, indicating the rocking chair again—with her elbow this time, because she was now holding the baby.

She waited until Lucas was seated.

"Here he is," she said, gently placing him into Lucas's arms. "Say hello to young Mr. Toomey."

Lucas smiled slightly. "A big boy," he said, glancing at Toomey. "Maybe he'll be a tribal cop—" He stopped, his voice sounding husky and strange. He looked down at the baby's face, stroking his cheek gently with one finger.

And then he began to speak to him softly in Navajo.

Toomey stood back, waiting respectfully for Lucas to give his blessing to his grandson. After a moment Lucas looked around at the nurse.

"I guess he has a schedule to keep," he said.

"Well, he does have an appointment to go see his mama," she answered.

Lucas leaned forward so that the nurse could take the

baby out of his arms, reaching out to touch him one last time before she took him away.

He stood and removed the paper gown.

"Toomey, you tell Eden—" he began as they stepped out into the hallway. "Tell Eden she—both of you—have a fine boy."

"I will, sir," Toomey said. "Are you sure you don't want to tell her yourself?"

"This is your time together now—the three of you. She and I can talk later." He started to walk away, but then he stopped.

"Toomey—" he said.

"Sir?"

"Take the day off."

Toomey grinned. "Yes, sir. I'll do that."

He was still smiling when he returned to Eden's room. She was asleep and didn't waken when the nurse wheeled the baby and his bassinet in.

"Just let her sleep," the nurse whispered. "Sloan's going to come in and check her in a little bit. She might as well rest until then."

He nodded and quietly moved his chair and the bassinet closer to the bed, so that both Eden and his son were within easy reach. He kept looking from one to the other. His wife and child. *His* family.

It had been a long, *long* journey from that hidden arroyo to here.

The baby began to fret, and he lifted him out of the bassinet and began rocking him gently, grateful for an excuse to hold him again.

"What's that you're humming, Ben?" Sloan said behind him.

"What?" he said, looking around at her.

"You were humming. It's nice. What is it?"

"Oh, I don't know," he said, but he did. He was humming the first song his and Eden's baby should hear.

He was humming "Tenderly."

* * * * *

Look for Cheryl Reavis's
emotional and moving Special Edition,
A CRIME OF THE HEART

to be available in
THE FATHER FACTOR *collection from*
By Request.
In stores April 1998!

and

Don't miss Cheryl's next
Silhouette Special Edition—
a THAT'S MY BABY! title—
coming to you this spring!

RETURN TO WHITEHORN

Silhouette's beloved **MONTANA MAVERICKS** returns with brand-new stories from your favorite authors! Welcome back to Whitehorn, Montana—a place where rich tales of passion and adventure are unfolding under the Big Sky. The new generation of Mavericks will leave you breathless!

Coming from Silhouette Special Edition°:

February 98: LETTER TO A LONESOME COWBOY by Jackie Merritt

March 98: WIFE MOST WANTED by Joan Elliott Pickart

May 98: A FATHER'S VOW by Myrna Temte

June 98: A HERO'S HOMECOMING by Laurie Paige

And don't miss these two very special additions to the Montana Mavericks saga:

MONTANA MAVERICKS WEDDINGS
by Diana Palmer, Ann Major and Susan Mallery
Short story collection available April 98

WILD WEST WIFE by Susan Mallery
Harlequin Historicals available July 98

Round up these great new stories
at your favorite retail outlet.

Silhouette®   Look us up on-line at: http://www.romance.net

SSEMMF-J

SUSAN MALLERY

Continues the twelve-book series—36 HOURS—in January 1998 with Book Seven

THE RANCHER AND THE RUNAWAY BRIDE

When Randi Howell fled the altar, she'd been running for her life! And she'd kept on running—straight into the arms of rugged rancher Brady Jones. She knew he had his suspicions, but how could she tell him the truth about her identity? Then again, if she ever wanted to approach the altar in earnest, how could she not?

For Brady and Randi and *all* the residents of Grand Springs, Colorado, the storm-induced blackout was just the beginning of 36 Hours that changed *everything!* You won't want to miss a single book.

Available at your favorite retail outlet.

SILHOUETTE WOMEN KNOW ROMANCE WHEN THEY SEE IT.

And they'll see it on **ROMANCE CLASSICS**, the new 24-hour TV channel devoted to romantic movies and original programs like the special **Romantically Speaking—Harlequin™ Goes Prime Time.**

Romantically Speaking—Harlequin™ Goes Prime Time introduces you to many of your favorite romance authors in a program developed exclusively for Harlequin® and Silhouette® readers.

Watch for **Romantically Speaking—Harlequin™ Goes Prime Time** beginning in the summer of 1997.

If you're not receiving ROMANCE CLASSICS, call your local cable operator or satellite provider and ask for it today!

Escape to the network of your dreams.

See Ingrid Bergman and Gregory Peck in *Spellbound* on Romance Classics.

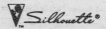